J. T. EDSON'S
FLOATING OUTFIT

The toughest bunch of Rebels that ever lost a war, they fought for the South, and then for Texas, as the legendary Floating Outfit of "Ole Devil" Hardin's O. D. Connected ranch.

MARK COUNTER was the best-dressed man in the West: always dressed fit-to-kill. BELLE BOYD was as deadly as she was beautiful, with a "Manhattan" model Colt tucked under her long skirts. THE YSABEL KID was Comanche fast and Texas tough. And the most famous of them all was DUSTY FOG, the ex-cavalryman known as the Rio Hondo Gun Wizard.

J. T. Edson has captured all the excitement and adventure of the raw frontier in this magnificent Western series. Turn the page for a complete list of Berkley Floating Outfit titles.

J.T. EDSON

THE WILDCATS

BERKLEY BOOKS, NEW YORK

Originally published in Great Britain by
Brown Watson Ltd.

THE WILDCATS

A Berkley Book / published by arrangement with
Transworld Publishers, Ltd.

PRINTING HISTORY
Corgi edition published 1969
Berkley edition / March 1981

ISBN: 0–425–04755–5

A BERKLEY BOOK ® TM 757,375

Berkley Books are published by Berkley Publishing Corporation,
200 Madison Avenue, New York, New York 10016.
PRINTED IN THE UNITED STATES OF AMERICA

THE WILDCATS

PART ONE

Better Than Calamity

THE TOWN'S USUAL crowd of loafers gathered at the Wells Fargo office to welcome the arrival of the west-bound stage. They watched the bouncing Concord stage roll to a halt, then waited to see who travelled aboard the coach. This day trade appeared to be bad, for only one passenger climbed down, a woman.

In height she stood at most five foot four. A dainty, small and stylish hat sat her piled-up red hair. The good ladies of the crowd whispered amongst themselves that the hair must be tinted with henna, although this might have been no more than their catty way with anyone better favored in the matter of looks than themselves. Her face looked attractive, maybe not out and out beautiful, but still pleasant, with lips which looked like they were used to smiling, and sparkling blue eyes. She wore a black travelling outfit, stylish, costly and in good taste. It did tend to emphasize her plump build, but plumpness, especially the type which sported a large bosom, reasonably slender waist and full hips, was held to be the peak of feminine attraction in male eyes at this time.

Her arrival stirred some speculation amongst the crowd, the more so as she appeared to be meaning to stay in Tennyson for some time. While they watched her baggage, including a large trunk, unloaded, the crowd speculated as to who she might be and why she came to their sleepy little Texas township. A variety of answers sprang to mind. That she was a rich widow come west to find a husband. She might be on the run from the law

3

after some spectacular crime back east. Or she might, studying her calm poised assurance and good clothes, be a famous theatrical lady on a tour, although that did not explain why she stopped in Tennyson which boasted only one saloon and it rarely imported entertainment.

They all studied the woman as eagerly as she ignored them, being more concerned with the unloading of her baggage. The women, still in their catty way, decided her age must be at least forty even though she looked in her middle thirties at most.

From the pile of bags which heaped around the trunk, the woman took a small grip. She stepped to where the Wells Fargo agent stood signing the driver's official delivery receipt book.

"Can you have my gear taken to the Bull's Head, Oscar?" she asked.

"B-Bull's Head?" squawked the agent, a thin, studious looking man whose name might well have been, but was not, Oscar. He heard the talk well up amongst the loafers at her words. "But that's a saloon, ma'am."

"I knew that when I bought it."

She made her reply with calm assurance, in the manner of a woman who knew her way around and cared little for the type of public opinion expressed by the people who stood around the front of the Wells Fargo office.

The watching and listening crowd stood, stared and talked amongst themselves discussing the woman's statement. A small group of dried-up, vinegar faced women; wives, mothers, unmarried sisters or spinsters; gathered like vultures over a kill, clucking their tongues, shaking their heads and mumbling together.

"Disgusting!"

"Shocking!"

"How could she!"

"This is a disgrace!"

If the red-haired woman heard the words – and they

were repeated often or spoken loud enough for her to do so – she ignored them. After throwing a cool, contemptuous look at the women and seeing them for what they were, she dismissed them as being of no importance to her future.

"Take hold of that bag there, Charlie," she said with easy familiarity to one of the loafers, indicating the top piece of luggage. "Tote it to the Bull's Head and there'll be drinks all night for you tonight."

Although he noted an expression of disapproval amongst the crowd of women, the man eagerly grabbed the bag. He grunted as he felt its weight, but gritted his teeth manfully and set into the task of toting the bag and keeping pace with the red-head. With the looks of the good ladies of Tennyson bouncing unheeded from her back, she walked along the street, keeping from the warped sidewalk the better to study her surroundings. Her bag-carrier struggled gamely by her side, trying to impress her with his strength.

"You aim to run the Bull's Head yourself, ma'am?" he asked, gasping the words out.

"I reckon so."

"It's a tough joint. Reckon it got too much for Turner. That's why he sold out."

For all the notice the woman took she might never have heard a word he said. Her eyes studied the length of Tennyson's main street in one quick glance and then appeared to dismiss it. Not that Tennyson looked any better, or had anything more to offer than a thousand other such small towns which dotted the open range country from the east line of Texas to the Pacific Ocean. The building materials might differ, ranging from stone and logs in the north to pure adobe or adobe and wood in the south. The names on the business premises might change. Yet the layout still looked the same with the same kind of businesses, the bank, the undertaker's shop, the saddler's place of work, stores, town marshal's office and jail, saloon, all in one way or another catering for the cowhand workers of the land.

She saw all this, but mostly her attention fixed on the Bull's Head Saloon. It looked to be a fair and substantial piece of structure, two floors high, with a veranda and rail for the upper floor's rooms, allowing their occupants a chance to step out into the fresh air without needing to walk downstairs. The lower floor looked much as the front of any other saloon. A hitching rail lined the sidewalk edge. The big front windows were painted white over their lower halves so that minors could not see their elders enjoying the pleasures within. The batwing doors gave a main entrance into the barroom.

The red-haired woman looked at all this with the expression of a pilgrim getting his first sight of the promised land, or an immigrant seeing the shores of America for the first time.

"Who's your great seizer?" she asked.

"Huh?" gasped the man, not sure he had heard right.

"Lawman, town marshal, county sheriff, whatever you have here."

"Tune Counter, ma'am," the man replied, wondering where this woman with her refined eastern clothes learned a western term for a law enforcement officer.

"He all right?"

"He's square enough, ma'am. Tried to make Turner run an honest place."

Giving a grunt which might have meant anything, the woman paused for a moment to give the saloon a last long searching look. Then she stepped on to the sidewalk, crossing it with purposeful stride and thrust open the batwing doors.

On the first glance the Bull's Head did not look prosperous or busy. At the bar two waiters and a bartender idly matched throws with dice. Half a dozen girls in dresses with left arms, shoulders and half the swell of their bosoms bare to view and ended just below their knees, sat around a table talking to themselves. So far there did not appear to be a single customer in the big barroom. The faro layout had a cover over its tiger-decorated top, the vingt-un and chuck-a-luck outfits stood silent and unused and the wheel of fortune on its stand by the wall did not spin. For the rest of it, the long bar's mirror showed no reflection of trade in progress and the shelves had few bottles on them. The doors leading to the outside world, the back rooms and the owner's private office, were all closed and the stairs leading to the first floor lay silent.

"Four fours to beat," said the bartender, from his place on the sober side of the counter. Then he threw a glance at the batwing doors to see who entered at this unexpected hour. He dropped the dice cup to the counter, staring at the door. The expression on his face brought every other eye to the entrance and the shape standing just inside.

"Excuse me, ma'am," one of the waiters said. "You got the wrong place. The hotel's down the street a piece, this-here's a saloon."

"I didn't buy it for a church-hall," replied the red-haired woman, walking forward and looking around with some interest.

At their table the girls stared. The big, good looking blonde's story of how she had been in Quiet Town during the wild days before Dusty Fog tamed it, died on her lips. She studied the newcomer with cold and calculating eyes. She saw the others looking at her and read their challenge for her to get up and do something. Shoving back her chair, she rose to meet the challenge. Then she stepped before the red-head with insolence showing in every inch of her frame.

An expectant, tense air filled the room. The workers and the townsman who carried the red-head's bag all knew Viola to be a real tough cookie and the boss-girl by the combined virtue of her skill in a hair-yanking brawl and having been Turner's girl-friend before he left. Viola had been treated with some favor under Turner's wing and she doubted if the same would apply with a female boss.

"You bought this place, did you?" she asked, planting herself full in the other woman's path, standing with hands on hips and legs braced apart, between the red-head and the bar.

Slowly the woman looked Viola up and down. Just as slowly she swung the grip on to the nearest table.

"I did."

"Well I don't like the idea of taking orders from a dame."

"Don't, huh?"

Speaking mildly and giving no warning of what she aimed to do, the red-head gave her employees a sign of how things would be run in the future. Her right hand folded into a fist and came around fast. She swung the fist like she knew what she was doing. It drove around, she dropped her shoulder behind the blow as it smashed with the power of a mule-kick against the side of Viola's jaw.

In his time the bardog had seen many a beautiful punch thrown and that right swing handed out by the red-head was as good as any he had seen from woman or man.

It landed well and squarely, spun Viola around on her heels, propelled her across the room to crash into the bar. Viola hung there for a moment, eyes glassy and mouth hanging open. Then slowly she slid to the floor, hanging with one arm draped over the brass foot-rail.

A stunned silence followed the crack of the blow and Viola's involuntary trip to the bar. Everyone in the room watched as the red-head took up her bag and crossed to where Viola sprawled in a limp pile on the floor. For a moment they expected the woman to drive a high-buttoned shoe into Viola's unprotected body. She did no such thing.

Placing her grip on the bar, the red-head bent and

hauled Viola away from the foot-rail and turned her face up. Then she looked at the bartender and said:

"Have you a bucket of water back there, Henry?"

"Yes'm," he replied, deciding this was not the time to point out his name was Sam.

Reaching down he lifted the bucket of water used for washing the glasses during business hours. He placed it on the bar-top from whence the woman lifted it one-handed, making no strain of it even though the full bucket weighed heavy. She gripped the bucket by handle and bottom, then up-ended it, pouring the water over Viola's head and shoulders.

With a gasp, followed by a spluttering squeal, Viola recovered and forced herself into a sitting position. Her head spun and she put a hand to a jaw which felt a good three times its normal size. Then she sniffed and started to wail in pain and humiliation.

The red-head bent forward, dug a hand into Viola's soaking hair and lifted her to her feet, then shoved her back against the bar. Hands on hips the newcomer studied Viola.

"The name's Madam Bulldog," said the red-head. "I'm your new boss. Got it?"

For a moment Viola clung to the bar, sniffing tears and staring at the other woman. Viola might have always been the boss' favorite and real tough in her own right, but she knew when to yell 'calf rope' and surrender. From the look of her, Madam Bulldog was more than ready and willing to wade in tooth and claw, or with those same hard fists to prove her point and make sure Viola 'got it'. After one sample Viola wanted no more.

"I got it," she mumbled through a jaw which hurt when she spoke.

Madam Bulldog turned to face the other girls, looking them over in the same impersonal manner.

"Anybody else need convincing?"

"No ma'am," answered the girls in chorus. They had

seen Viola yell, "calf rope" and needed no more convincing.

Turning once more to the bar Madam Bulldog looked around her. "Where did Turner room?" she asked.

"I'll show you," Viola replied, working on the sound principle of "If you can't lick 'em, join 'em."

"I want to see all that staff here in a couple of hours," Madam told the bartender. "Who's been running things since Turner left?"

"I have," replied the bartender, thinking of the profit which slipped into his pocket since Turner departed the scene hurriedly and wondering if she would find out about it.

"Then I want to see you and the books in the office when I come down," she said and pointed to the man who carried her bags. "See that gent has free drinks all night tonight."

With that she turned and nodded to Viola who led her upstairs. Viola looked a little guilty and worried as she opened the door to Turner's room, for her belongings lay scattered about.

"I used it after Joe – Mr. Turner left," she said.

"And while he was here, I wouldn't be surprised," answered Madam Bulldog dryly. "And don't try to look shocked or innocent. If you're innocent, I am; and it'd take a damned sight more than that to shock me. Get your gear cleared out this afternoon so I can move in. And I'd better know your name."

"Viola."

"You're the boss girl?"

"I was," agreed Viola, a trifle bitter at her loss of face and station in life.

"You still are. You'll get ten dollars a week over the pay the other girls make and you'll earn it. I expect you to keep the girls in line and see there's no trouble. None of you roll drunks, go on the streets, or make fuss with the town women. Can you handle it?"

Viola nodded. She had never been paid extra, nor had

any special duties under Turner's control. However, she reckoned she would be able to handle things the way her new boss wanted them handling.

"Then make a start at clearing the room out," said Madam Bulldog. "I'll move in after I've attended to a few things."

Saying this Madam Bulldog turned and headed downstairs once more, still carrying her small grip. She went straight to the office, halted at the door to tell the waiters to close the main doors and keep customers out, then went inside to interview the sweating bartender. He indicated the safe, its door standing open, and the books which lay on the desk top ready for her inspection.

"I only want to get an idea of what trade Turner did here," she remarked. "I expect you made a reasonable profit out of running things. And don't look so pained, you'd have been a fool not to. I only bought the building and fittings. From what I can see you ran the place all right so you're welcome to whatever you made. If you want a drink, go get one. Then let's talk."

It became clear that Madam Bulldog knew more than a little about running a saloon. She asked pertinent questions about trade, the customers, sources of liquor supplies, how they stood with the local citizens. She also discovered the bartender's name to be Sam, not Henry.

"I don't want any customer to complain of short measure, short change, spiked drinks or anything," she warned at the end of her check. "You order what fresh liquor supplies we need this afternoon. Now let's take a look at the games."

Her inspection of the decks of cards proved she knew more than a little about such things. She examined the cards, studying the designs on their backs, then riffling them through her fingers, watching the designs flip by and alert for any sign of irregularity which would warn her the cards had been marked.

One thing caught Madam Bulldog's eye immediately,

the cards lay in two separate piles. After her inspection she waved a hand to the left hand pile.

"Get rid of 'em," she ordered, watching the bartender's face and ready to take action if he objected.

"Sure, boss," Sam replied instantly and in a manner which told her he had nothing to do with the ownership of the cards.

She threw a look at the small group of workers who sat around, seeing they all watched her with interest but not animosity. They most likely wondered what changes she intended to make and how those changes would affect them.

"Who handles the gambling, Sam?" she asked.

"Feller called Wallace. Took a percentage cut with Turner."

"I hope he's another place marked down," she said quietly.

They went to the chuck-a-luck table but Madam's thorough inspection found nothing in either its operation of dice to meet with her disapproval although the layout of numbers needed their odds corrected to give the players a fair chance. The Vingt-un layouts needed only honest decks of cards to make them satisfactory. However, the wheel of fortune had a concealed control button connected to springs and wires which took all the chance from its operation as far as the house was concerned. A quick rip tore the wires loose and Sam beat his boss to the move. Madam Bulldog nodded her agreement and they headed for the faro layout.

Once more Madam Bulldog showed her remarkable knowledge of such matters. She gave the dealer's box on the table a careful inspection, then stepped back and looked at the table itself, seeing how thick and stoutly made it looked to be. She bent and examined the end where the dealer sat by the case keeping box. Her hands ran along the wood and a panel in the side slid open. With a grunt as if she expected no more, Madam Bulldog removed a second box, one which looked almost the same as the one on the table. Yet it contained certain improvements the box on the table did not have, by far the most important being that the slot through which the cards could be dealt had room for two cards instead of one to pass.

With a grunt she raised one box in each hand, then smashed them down against the table edge, shattering them. Tossing the wrecked boxes to the floor she went on:

"I'll not have a second dealer box in my house, Sam. When my bags get here I've a straight box, with an open top."

Sam caught the significance of the remark. The two boxes she broke did not have their tops left open, but only a small hole through which the cards could be pushed. The second dealer box allowed the manipulator to put two cards out, then retract the top one if having it played would not be favorable to the house.

"We have a swamper?" she asked.

"Two, they're not here now."

"I want to see them. I want this floor washed every day before we open and fresh sawdust on it."

"I'll see to it," Sam promised.

"Swell," she said. "Where's the bank?"

"Down the street. Only the banker's wife wouldn't let Turner do any business in it."

The news did not appear to distress Madam Bulldog. She waved the hand holding the grip towards the door.

"Let's go see him."

Her interview with the banker proved once and for all to Sam that Madam Bulldog could take care of herself in any society. She swept aside the protesting teller and entered Banker Hoscroft's private office with Sam following on her heels.

Before the banker could rise and impose his full pompous power upon her, Madam Bulldog dumped the grip before him and opened it.

"There's five thousand dollars in here," she said calmly, as if she wished to deposit five dollars. "I've a further fifteen thousand in the First Union Bank in Kansas City. You can have it here in my account, or I'll open my own bank. It's all up to you."

Despite his present position in life, and his pompous manner – which was mainly due to marrying a Bostonian lady – Banker Hoscroft was a shrewd man of business. A deposit of twenty thousand dollars would do his bank nothing but good. He might let his wife dictate to him on some matters, but could also put his foot firmly down when necessary. So he donned his most jovial smile and the manner he reserved for his largest depositors, escorted Madam Bulldog to the business section of the building and opened an account for her.

"I'll be expecting to see you in for my grand opening tonight," she said as she left the bank and Hoscroft agreed he would be there.

From the bank Madam Bulldog passed around the town, visiting such businesses as she would need to deal with, leaving each place with the owners full of admiration for her astute business sense. The owners of the businesses saw they would make profit far in excess of anything Turner put their way and that was one argument to silence the objections of wives, mothers, spinster sister or maiden aunts who might complain.

Actually the complaints never came. Seeing a meeting of the good ladies in the Black Cat Café, Madam Bulldog bearded them in their den. She stated quite firmly she aimed to run her place, but also promised that the conducting of it would be blameless. She spoke to such effect that not only did the ladies withhold their complaints but they accepted her as a social equal.

All the saloon's employees were waiting to meet their new boss. Sam noticed an expectant air and looked to where Wallace, a small sly man in the usual dress of a frontier gambler, stood by the faro layout and scowling at the wrecked dealing boxes. Wallace turned, looked towards Madam Bulldog and came to meet her, a truculent gleam in his eye. He waved a hand towards the broken boxes which he dropped on the table top.

"Did you do that?" he asked in a threatening manner.

"I did."

"Why, you fat—!"

That was when Madam Bulldog hit him. She ripped a punch into his belly, just under the watch chain on his fancy vest. It came so unexpectedly and with such power that it folded Wallace over, right on to the other hand as it came up, knotted into a useful fist, to meet his jaw. He straightened out again and went sprawling on to his back, cursing, spitting blood and clawing at the butt of the Second Model Smith & Wesson revolver under his jacket.

"I can copper that bet, too."

Madam Bulldog gave the warning in a flat, cold voice. She held a Colt Cloverleaf House Pistol in her right hand, drawn from under her coat in a flickering blur of movement. Before Wallace could collect his scattered wits, or get his gun out, the .41 calibre barrel lined on him, the two exposed cylinders of the "cloverleaf" chamber like two unwinking eyes watching him.

While being a real mean cuss and card cheat, Wallace also had a wide yellow streak in him. He knew better than to call the bet when the other side held a .41 calibre, four shot answer to his play. He let his hand come clear of the gun and backed away, crawling across the floor, fingers feeling at his jaw.

"Have you got a horse?" asked Madam Bulldog.

"Yeah!" Wallace replied in what he hoped would be a defiant snarl, but that came out more of a whine.

"Then get on it and be out of town before the marshal gets back or I'll show him those decks of cards and tell him why I bust the dealing boxes."

She knew she had won, even without meeting Tune

Counter. It showed in the scared expression which came in Wallace's eyes and on his hate-lined face. She guessed the town marshal had been interested in Wallace's little additions to luck without being able to prove what they were. In which case Wallace would not be around when the marshal came back that evening.

"See him on his way, Sam," she ordered.

Sam needed no second bidding. He had never approved of swindling the customers, regarding it at best as a short-sighted policy which eventually led to trouble with both the customers and the law. He knew Tune Counter would never stand for any crooked play if he detected it and had long expected the marshal to catch Wallace out, then close the saloon down.

Bending forward Sam grabbed Wallace by the jacket collar and hauled him to his feet then hustled him across the room to the side door. One of the waiters, who felt the same way as did Sam on the subject of crooked gamblers, obligingly opened the door through which Wallace departed, helped on his way by a hard-applied boot.

"Git – and keep going!" Sam advised.

Wallace took the hint. He saw that his presence in the saloon would no longer be tolerated. So he headed for his room at the hotel to collect his belongings. If he nursed a grudge against Madam Bulldog and her employees he did not intend to stay around and do anything about it.

The teller at Hoscroft's bank beamed a welcome to Madam Bulldog as she entered through the doors at eleven o'clock on a warm summer's morning something over a year after her arrival in Tennyson.

"Good morning, Madam," he greeted, using the only name by which anyone in town knew her. He reached for the canvas bag she laid on the counter before him. "You look to have been busy last night."

"Fair enough," she replied, then turned to Marshal

Tune Counter as he stood by the teller's cage. "Hi, Tune. You putting it in too?"

"Sure," he replied. "I get paid the same day as the cowhands. My pile looks sort of paltry besides your's though."

She laughed. "You don't have my overheads."

They got on very well together, the marshal and the saloon-keeper. In fact romance had been increasingly hinted at, for he spent some of his time with her and not in duty hours. Certainly Tune liked her, admired her for the way she kept her promise of allowing the place to run smoothly and fairly, relying on the house percentage to make the gambling pay. Nor did Madam ever offend the public good taste by appearing on the streets in her working clothes. To see her around town one might never have known she ran a saloon, for she always dressed in stylish and conventional fashion.

"The trouble with my business," she went on, "is—"

The words died on her lips. Behind them the door of the bank had opened and four men stepped inside, fanning across it as it closed once more. Madam Bulldog glanced to see who might be entering, then stood very still, her words dying away unsaid. Tune Counter stood just as still, his hands on the teller's counter top and well clear of the Army Colt at his side. Behind the counter, the teller stayed just where he was. He gave a quick look at the Navy Colt kept under the counter for just such emergencies, but he made no attempt to touch it.

Not with four men standing across the room and lining guns on him and the two customers. Four tall, trail-dirty, mean-looking men. At least eyes held a mean glint, being about all of their faces which showed from behind the drawn-up bandana masks. They handled their weapons like they knew which end the flame came out of. The clothes they wore, even without the dirt, would have been hard to describe and no different to those worn by thousands of cowhands. Except that this bunch were not any kind of cowhands, but master at a line of business perfected by Mr. Jesse and Frank James of Clay County, Missouri.

From the way the four men stood and acted they had not just started on this line of business, but knew it from A to izzard. A man couldn't take foolish chances with that kind, not and stay alive to boast about it.

"Just stand there nice and easy," ordered the man at the right. "That way we won't have any fuss. Now turn around real slow, the lady first."

On turning, Madam Bulldog studied the four men, not trying to memorize details about them, but to see what sort of opposition she might have to tie into. She saw one of them would be the real danger. The other three looked like older men, competent workers who conducted their business quickly and with as little rough stuff as possible. The fourth was young. His eyes bore a look which told he wanted nothing more than an excuse to throw lead.

"All right, big feller," said the man at the right. "Now you."

Tune obeyed. He had no intention of making a move or trying to go against the guns of the four men. Not that Tune was a coward. He had proved his courage on every occasion which demanded it. But a lawman needed to know when to stand fast as well as when to make his gun-play. To make it now would endanger the lives of Madam Bulldog and the bank teller.

Only the matter left Tune's hand the moment he turned far enough for the youngster at the left of the quartet to see his badge. A low snarl rippled the masking bandana and he swung his gun around. Tune Counter saw the move and flung himself to one side, right hand stabbing at his Army Colt. Flame tore from the young outlaw's gun and Tune took a .36 calibre ball in the left shoulder, went to his knees but got his gun out.

"You fool k—!" yelled one of the others.

Then all hell tore loose in the bank. Madam Bulldog's

right hand went under her coat in a fast move. The men had discounted her as a factor until too late. Flame spurted from the Colt Cloverleaf and a hole appeared between the youngster's eyes, slamming him around the instant before he could trigger another shot into the marshal. He hit the man next to him, knocking his gun out of line even as he tried to bring it around and cope with the new menace.

Although hit in the left shoulder Tune Counter drew his gun with the right hand, throwing lead into the man at the right and spinning him into the wall. However, the man still held his gun and Tune acted in the manner of a trained law enforcement officer. While the man still held his gun he could be termed dangerous, so Tune shot him again. At the same moment another of the bunch sent a bullet into Tune. The outlaw did not get a chance to take another shot for the teller grabbed up his Navy Colt and fired. His actions might have been in the nature of a concerned rat, knowing it to be a case of fight or die. This made the gun in his hand no less deadly although more luck than skill sent home the bullet which dropped the outlaw.

The fourth man, seeing his three pards go down, forgot fighting. He made a leap for the door, throwing it open and darting out. The shots had aroused interest and brought people out, people holding guns, for this was a Texas town and every man in it owned a firearm of some kind. Making for the waiting horses, the man made a leapfrog mount aboard his mount as it turned from the hitching rail. He set the pet-makers to work and ran the gauntlet of fire along the street, lead singing around his ears.

He almost made it through without a scratch, then his luck gave out. The agent for the Wells Fargo office cut loose with a short barrelled guard's model ten gauge shotgun. The nine buckshot charge had spread some and the outlaw took three balls in his back. He yelled in agony but managed to stay in his saddle. After the lapse his luck returned. Not only did he manage to keep on his horse but no posse followed him, for the town was disorganized without Tune Counter's strong hand to guide them. The outlaw rode for all that day, through the night and late the following morning dropped unconscious before the door of a rancher who made far more money hiding outlaws than by working his cattle.

In Tennyson, even while the guns roared, Madam Bulldog went to Tune Counter and dropped to her knees by him. She looked at the teller who retained enough of his senses to go forward and disarm the three outlaws.

"Get the doctor!" she ordered.

The teller needed no second order, he went outside and yelled for medical aid. Madam Bulldog stayed by Tune, not touching or moving him. She could see he was in pain, but he stayed conscious and his instincts were those of a lawman. He looked at the three sprawled out forms on the floor and weakly pointed.

"That one's still alive," he said. "See to him."

"Let him rot," Madam Bulldog answered. "I'm seeing to you."

Not until the doctor, followed by the teller, entered, did she go to the wounded outlaw. He was dying and nothing could save him, or could have saved him had she gone to him immediately. His eyes went to her face and he pointed to the youngster who brought the trouble on them.

"That damned fool kid!" he gasped. "He was kill crazy. Worse than the other Cousins boys."

Madam Bulldog felt as if a cold hand touched her. She looked down at the dying outlaw and asked. "Is *he* one of the Cousins family?"

"Yeah. He was Breck. Hank Cousins' youngest."

Turning her face towards Tune Counter, the woman saw he had both heard and understood. This in itself was not surprising, most everybody in Texas had heard of the Cousins family. They were a close-knit clan of a father and four sons – only now but three sons remained. The fourth son's lifeless body lay on the floor of the Tennyson bank, a .41 calibre hole in his forehead, the back of his skull a bloody, brain-spattered, bone-shattered horror where the bullet smashed out again.

The Cousins family, Hank, the father, a balding, heavily built man with some pretensions at being educated and peering through steel rimmed spectacles at the world, Joe, Tad and Burt, had the reputation of being bad-men, killers with no regard for human life. A sullen wolf-pack full of hate, with but one redeeming quality, their loyalty to each other. Cut one Cousins and the whole stinking brood bled. Now one of their kin had died at the hands of the people of Tennyson, or a section of the population. The rest of the clan would not rest easy, when they heard, until they shed blood, killed whoever shot down Breck and all who might have been near when it happened.

"You mean that there's Breck Cousins," gasped the teller, having returned in time to hear the outlaw's words.

"The late and not lamented," replied Madam Bulldog.

Behind her the doctor glared at Tune Counter as he tried to force himself to his feet.

"Lie down again, Tunc!" he spat. "You'll kill yourself afore I get a chance to do it."

"What about the other man?" Tune replied.

"He got clear, carrying lead," growled the doctor. "Now lie easy, blast you, and let me fix those wounds."

Tune shook his head weakly, still trying to rise. He had his duty to the town, to the badge he wore. Sooner or later, depending on if the wounded man lived or died, word would reach the Cousins clan, the escaped outlaw would bear the word; or the prairie telegraph carry it. Then the Cousins bunch would be riding, hunting the man who killed Breck. That it had been Madam Bulldog not a man who shot him, that she shot in defence of another man's life, would mean nothing to the family.

They had killed women before and done worse before
killing. Tune knew he must get help, bring in a reliable
man or men into town to stiffen the citizens and help
guard Madam Bulldog until he could stand on his feet
again.

He thought of men who would willingly offer their
help. Most of them were occupied on law enforcement
work from which they could not easily be spared,
although they would come willingly if he asked. He
thought of another man, a member of his own family, a
nephew.

"Hold it, Doc!" he gasped, then beckoned Madam
Bulldog to his side. "Happen you want to stay alive.
Send a telegraph message – to Old Devil – Hardin. Tell
him what happened here!"

He had been three days in the saddle, riding north
from the great OD Connected ranch in the Rio Hondo
country, headed for the small town of Tennyson in Sand
County. Soon it would be night again and he must
spend it sage-henning out under the stars, something he
never took kindly to doing no matter that he spent a
good half of his life sleeping in such a manner. Around
noon the next day he ought to reach Tennyson and
discover the meaning of the telegraph message which
brought him away from the urgent business of gathering
a shipping herd for delivery to a fort that had trouble
feeding hungry Kiowa tribesmen. It had been almost
three years since he last saw his Uncle Tune and so he
wondered what need the marshal of Tennyson might
have for his services.

Sitting his seventeen hand bloodbay stallion with the
easy grace of a light rider despite his giant size, Mark
Counter presented a picture Fred Remington or any
other artist would not have hesitated to set on canvas.

Six foot three, even without the aid of his expensive,
made-to-measure, fancy stitched boots, he stood and
with the physique of a Hercules. His shoulders had a

great spread to them, his frame trimmed down to a lean waist and long, powerful legs. Yet in no way did he look slow, clumsy, or awkward, exactly the opposite in fact, and he sat his horse in a manner which took less out of it than would a lighter though less skilled rider.

His costly white Stetson hat, with its silver concha decorated band, sat on neatly barbered golden blond hair. The face, shielded by the wide brim of the low crowned hat, looked almost classically handsome, tanned, intelligent, virile and with strength of character etched upon it. In appearance he looked much like a Greek god of old who elected to wear the dress of a cowhand instead of his formal robes. In all things Mark tended to be a dandy dresser. His tan colored shirt had been tailored for him, as had the levis trousers which hung with turned back cuffs outside his boots. The tight rolled green bandana around his throat and trailing long ends over his shirt was made of pure silk. Once the Beau Brummel of the Confederate cavalry, now Mark's dress style tended to set cowhand fashion in Texas.

Around his waist hung a gunbelt with a brace of fine looking ivory handled 1860 Army Colts riding in holsters that looked just right and told a story to eyes which knew the signs. The entire rig, expensive though it was, looked both functional and practical, the kind of outfit a real fast man with a gun would wear.

Mark Counter could lay just claim to being a fast man with a gun. There was more than just a dandy dresser to him. He knew the cattle business from calf down to shipping pen and acknowledged no superior at the cowhand trade. His strength had become a legend and his skill in a roughhouse brawl talked of wherever it had been seen. He could handle a rifle well, though not as well as his good *amigo* the Ysabel Kid. He could handle his matched guns very well, although not quite as well as his illustrious *amigo*, Dusty Fog. Reliable witnesses, men who themselves were no slouches at the art of getting them out and throwing lead through them, claimed

Mark Counter ran Dusty Fog a close second in speed and accuracy. The general public, however, knew little of this, for Mark rode in the shadow of the fastest of them all, the Rio Hondo gun wizard called Dusty Fog.

This day, and for the past two days, Mark Counter rode alone. The OD Connected had been very busy and, while Ole Devil would have spared the whole of the floating outfit if need be, Mark suggested he rode alone. On reaching Tennyson he would discover why his Uncle Tune needed his aid. If he then decided the situation called for more men he could send a telegraph message which would bring Dusty Fog, the Ysabel Kid and Red Blaze hot-foot to his aid.

An ear splitting "splat!" sounded just over Mark's head, a sound he knew all too well. The sound of a close passing bullet as it split the air above him. Even as he heard the crack of the shot to his left Mark went sideways from the saddle to the right. He landed on his feet, holding his right hand Colt with the hammer drawn back ready to use and with the bloodbay between himself and the shooter.

Mark peered cautiously around the horse's neck and across the range. The shot appeared to have came from the small clump of trees out about a hundred yards away; which did not make Mark feel any happier with his present situation. His rifle remained in the saddleboot and the problem would be how to get it from the left side without taking a bullet between his shoulders in doing so. Sure he held the revolver. Sure an 1860 Army Colt would carry and kill at a hundred yards. But a man didn't like the idea of staking his life on it, not when matched against what sounded like a Winchester carbine. True the Winchester Model of 1866 used a comparatively light twenty-eight grain load, much the same as the Army Colt. The carbine, however, gave better range with its twenty inch barrel than did the Colt's eight inch barrel length.

Nothing stirred for a few seconds. Mark wondered

who might be shooting at him and why no further shots came. He gave some thought of how he might lure his unknown attacker into a range where the Army Colt could be used with accuracy and deadly effect.

"Yahoo," whooped a voice he knew all too well. "IIi, Mark. Mark Counter!"

Giving a disgusted grunt, Mark set his Colt's hammer on the safety notch and holstered the weapon. He swung into his saddle once more and saw that he guessed the direction of the shot correctly and the make of the gun. Calamity Jane rode from the clump of trees with her Winchester carbine resting across her arm.

In the years since Charlotte Canary left her family in the care of the St. Louis convent and faded for ever out of their lives, the eldest daughter, Martha Jane had travelled far and made something of a name for herself.

The last time Mark saw her she had been riding the box of a freight wagon, wearing an old buckskin jacket, patched pants, battered old hat and scuff-heeled boots. It appeared her fortunes had taken a turn for the better. Now she wore an expensive Texas style black Stetson hat sitting on her shortish, curly red hair. Her face had a tan, was still good looking, friendly and bore its usual reckless grin. She stood around five foot seven, her figure rich and full, maybe just a mite buxom but still firm fleshed and attractive. The rolled up sleeves of her tartan shirt showed arms a mite more muscular than a lady ought to have, but Calamity never set herself up as a lady. The tight rolled silk bandana hung long ends down between the full swell of bosom as the breasts strained against the shirt which hung open one button too many. The levis trousers looked like they had been bought a size too small the way they clung to and emphasized her full hips and thighs. Around her waist hung a new black gunbelt with an ivory butted Colt Navy revolver nestling in the fast draw holster, butt forward at the right side. On another woman this might have looked like an amusing affectation, but Mark knew Calamity could draw and shoot in just under a second and put lead into a man-sized target at gunfighting ranges at the end of that time.

Calamity charged forward and at the last moment swung her horse with the grace of a polo pony and halted it at the side of Mark's bloodbay stallion. The horse, a fancy, high-stepping buckskin stud, like Calamity's outfit, pointed to her affluence.

"Mark, you ole goat!" she said, booting the carbine and thrusting a hand out towards him. "Where you headed? Where's Cap'n Fog and the Kid? How you been keeping yourself, you ole coyote? See Belle Starr lately?"

"Ease off and let me answer one at a time," he replied, finding her hand felt as hard and strong as ever. "You look like you're in the money."

"You said it. I've been freighting for the army up north, but we paid off a piece back and some of the boys allowed they could play poker. Which same only goes to show, now don't it."

"Sure does," agreed Mark, knowing Calamity fancied her skill as a poker player. "Where're you headed, gal?"

"Down trail a piece, saw you coming and allowed to give you a surprise. Boy, you sure lit down from that hoss real *pronto*. Where're you making for?"

"Tennyson," Mark replied, hoping she would be hide-bound for some other town.

"Yahoo!" whooped Calamity. "Ain't this my lucky day. Here's me headed for Tennyson myself. We can ride in together."

Which was just about the last thing Mark wanted. In fact he could not think of anybody he would less want to head for Tennyson with. His uncle ran the law in Tennyson and needed help, most likely in some serious matter pertaining to his office. While Mark could not think why Calamity would be headed for Tennyson he did know one thing for sure, the visit would most likely wind up with trouble. Calamity's idea of fun was to ride in, find a saloon, locate its toughest female employee and pick a fight with her. If in doing this Calamity could also embroil the rest of the saloon in a general free-for-all it made her day and she enjoyed it to the full.

Not that Mark objected to a good fight and had been in more than one free-for-all in his time. Only right now he was on business, serious business, and a saloon ruckus came under the heading of pleasure. He knew that Calamity would do her damnedest to get him involved in a fight if she could, just to see him in action and admire his skill in a brawl.

"Why Tennyson, Calam?" he asked. "It's nothing but a sleepy lil one hoss town. I'd h've thought you'd be headed for Wichita."

"Nope, Tennyson," she replied, then as if it explained everything, "Madam Bulldog's there."

It explained plenty and Mark could have groaned at the words. He had overlooked the stories he heard about Madam Bulldog. Now he saw the reason for Calamity's visit and did not care for what he saw. It spelled but one thing – TROUBLE. Might even be the trouble he had been sent for to help handle although he doubted that. His Uncle Tune might not be a spring-chicken, but he could handle fuss between two women even if one of them be Calamity Jane.

"You heard of her?" Calamity asked after they had rode on in silence for a moment.

"Some," Mark replied.

"They say she can play better poker, out cuss, drink, shoot, fight and spit any woman around. Waal, she can't. Not while old Calamity Jane's still on her feet and r'aring to go."

Now Mark knew for sure what Calamity's intentions were. Like some men would ride out of their way to meet a fast gun and pick a fight with him, so Calamity Jane sought out, to try conclusions with, any tough woman she heard about. Calamity felt some pride in her toughness and the notoriety it brought her way. She laid claim to the same talents as legend had it Madam Bulldog showed, so what would be more natural but that Calamity would ride over to Tennyson and see who was the better woman.

Only this did not cause Mark to feel any happier about meeting Calamity. In a tight spot and when guns roared Mark would not object to Calamity at his side, for the girl had sand to burn and could handle her weapons. At a time like this, with some real urgent business on hand. Calamity was about as welcome as a rattlesnake in bed. Yet there didn't seem much he could do about it. Texas was a free country and Calamity could ride to Tennyson if she felt like it.

They rode on together. Towards dusk Calamity took her carbine from the saddleboot and blew the heads from four big jack rabbits which showed such poor sense as to halt in their flight within shooting range. Then as night closed in they headed for a small wood which gave them shelter and through which flowed a small stream. There they made camp. Like Mark, she carried her bedroll on her Cheyenne roll saddle but instead of a Manilla rope had her blacksnake whip strapped to its horn. Mark cared for the horses while she made a fire and prepared the meal. Give her credit, Calamity sure knew how to cook up a mess of rabbit meat in a way that would make a man's mouth water, Mark thought. She also made real good coffee in the true range tradition that a spoon should be able to stand upright in it.

After the meal they sat for a time talking over their last meeting and some of their mutual acquaintances. Calamity also talked of her forthcoming meeting with Madam Bulldog. She had heard of the saloonkeeper during her freighting trip and at its end prepared herself to enter the lists and toss down the gauntlet. Staking her pay in a poker game, she built it into a good-sized roll out of which she bought an eye-catching outfit, a new gunbelt and Colt and a fancy horse. She aimed to show folks what a real tough gal looked like.

"Well," Mark drawled. "I'm turning in now."

Taking his bedroll, Mark opened it out, spreading the seven by eighteen foot water-proof tarpaulin cover on the ground, exposing the two suggans, heavy patchwork quilts and a couple of blankets as well as his depleted war bag which contained ammunition and spare clothing.

Calamity came over and looked down at the top suggan which appeared to have been built around three gingham dresses, several garish frocks and various items of female underclothing.

"That the suggan you had made after the battle at Bearcat Annies,* Mark?" she asked.

"Sure is."

"From all I heard that was some cat-brawl. I wish I'd been along for it."

The incident to which Calamity referred had occurred while Mark served as Dusty Fog's deputy in the Montana gold camp called Quiet Town. Three female deputies went into Bearcat Annie's saloon to arrest the owner and create a diversion to allow the male members of the town's police force to enter and take a bunch of hired gunmen. Mark needed a new suggan at the time and had one made from the torn clothing. From the look of the suggan it had, as Calamity said, been some fight.

One thing Mark knew for sure. No matter how Calamity felt on the subject, the law in Quiet Town had had enough on its combined hands without her adding to its complications – just as he had right now.

"Yes sir, I'd sure liked to be there," sighed Calamity, sounding like a housewife wishing she could have attended some cooking contest. "What're you headed to Tennyson for, Mark?"

* Told in *Quiet Town*.

"Uncle Tune's the law up there. He sent a message he needed some help, so I came along."

"Sure pleased you did," she sighed. "Gets to be lonely, sage henning without company." She threw a glance at him. "I'm going to turn in."

"And me," Mark answered. "Good night, Calam."

Mark settled down, drawing the blanket and suggans over him but did not bother snapping the hooks and eyes of the tarp to make himself a waterproof cover, for the sky held no sign of rain. For a time he lay awake, listening to the night noises and the stamping of the horses. He wondered why his Uncle Tune might need him.

"Mark!" Calamity called from the other side of the fire.

"Yes?"

"I'm cold."

What could a Texas gentleman, raised in the traditions of Southern chivalry and hospitality, do? Could he allow a poor girl to lie shivering in cold through all the silent hours of the night?

He most certainly could not!

Rising to his feet, Mark carried his bedroll to where Calamity lay peeping up at him. He placed his own blankets on top of her and sat down.

A few minutes later Calamity whispered, "I'm so warm now I'll have to take this damned shirt off, Mark."

"That's the best idea you've had all day," he answered.

Calamity Jane sat on her blankets and looked across the clearing as she tucked the shirt into her trousers. By the stream Mark Counter stood shaving without the use of a mirror. He had removed his shirt for his morning ablutions and the rising sun's beams played on the muscles which writhed and moved under his tanned skin. Calamity got to her feet and gave a contented sigh.

"Yes sir, Martha Jane," she thought. "That Mark Counter's a real hunk of man for sure."

After breakfast, prepared by Calamity, they rode on once more. On the ride they talked of many things, but love was not one of the subjects they discussed. Neither Calamity nor Mark harbored any thoughts of romance, even after their interlude the previous night. Certainly she did not visualize herself dressed in white, looking virginal and bride-like before the altar and becoming Mrs. Mark Counter. She had known Mark for some time and counted him as being a good friend. Calamity always tried to be generous to her friends.

Shortly before noon they topped a ridge and received their first view of the town of Tennyson. Calamity let out a disgruntled curse as she studied the place, for it did not come up to her preconceived ideas.

"Huh!" she grunted in annoyance. "What a one hoss town. You reckon there *is* a Madam Bulldog, Mark?"

"*You* reckoned there was," he replied.

"That was before I saw Tennyson," she sniffed. "I'll bet she's nothing but some fat old calico cat who one time got lucky with a deck of cards. Still I've come this far, so I might as well ride the rest of the way. Might even be able to help you and your uncle out."

Mark did not reply to this. He doubted if his Uncle Tune would thank him for bringing Calamity along. However, Mark could think of no way to prevent her coming and so decided to make the best of a bad job.

A crowd gathered about the building which housed Doc Connel's home, office and what passed for a hospital in Tennyson. Some two dozen or so citizens stood in a sullen half circle before the outside flight of stairs which led up to Doc's office. In the front, acting as a leader of the people, stood Joe Stern, the local blacksmith and a man much admired for his strength, if for nothing else, around town.

Right at that moment Stern faced Connel like a bear confronted by a fighting cock. The description seemed very apt for Doc Connel stood little more than five foot six and had all the aggressive spirit of a game bird. No man in the town had ever succeeded in browbeating Doc or making him back water. From the look of things he did not aim to let them start this day.

"Now you listen to me, Doc!" Stern said in his most blustering manner. "It ain't that we don't respect Tune Counter. But them Cousins bunch sent a telegraph message sayings they's coming looking for him. And you knows what that means."

"I know what *you* bunch here are," Doc replied in his most hide-blistering and insulting tone. "I suppose if Hank Cousins told you to string Tune up from a cottonwood tree you'd do it."

A mutter of objection rose from the members of the crowd. None of them paid any attention to the two riders who came towards them, for all eyes were on their leader and the chief of the opposition to the 'run Tune Counter out of town' club.

"Now you know we wouldn't do that, Doc," Stern objected. "All we want to do is put ole Tune in a wagon and take him to Sand City where there's a sheriff and deputies and the cavalry at the Fort to protect him."

"Tune wouldn't make five miles in a wagon," Connel replied. "Which same Sand City's over fifty miles on bad roads. He stays!"

Neither Mark nor Calamity Jane had the slightest idea what the gathering might be about. They brought their horses to a halt and Mark raised his voice, cutting off the mutters of objection which rolled from the crowd.

"Excuse me, folks. Where at's Marshal Counter?"

The crowd turned their scared faces to him, taking in his matched Colts and general air of tough ability and handiness. They next looked Calamity over with some curiosity.

"Who's asking?" Stern asked, taking courage from the fact that none of the Cousins' bunch fitted Mark's description.

Swinging from his saddle, Mark walked forward. The crowd parted to let him pass through. Calamity stayed where she was, leaning forward on the horn of her Cheyenne roll saddle, watching all of them.

"I'm Tune Counter's nephew," Mark replied. "Where'd I find him?"

"You find him up here, friend," Connel answered, jerking a thumb over his shoulder. "Tune took lead a couple of days back. He's sick and sorry, but he's still living."

"And he's got the Cousins bunch after him," Stern went on, for once having to look up to a man. He weighed somewhat heavier than Mark, but stood two inches shorter. "You kin of his?"

"So my pappy allus told me."

"Then you talk some sense into Doc there!" yelled Stern, pointing to Connel. "Get Tune out of here and to Sand City afore the Cousins boys come in after him."

"I'll tell this feller what I told you, Stern," said Doc Connel calmly. "Old Tune's not fit to be moved for a week at least."

"Which means he stays right where he is," drawled Mark and stepped forward, meaning to go up and see his uncle.

Never before had Stern seen his wishes flouted in such a manner. He shot out a big hand to clamp on Mark's left bicep – and got himself a shock. Despite having been in the saddle for four days Mark's clothes still retained their costly, and rather dandy, appearance and his voice held the cultured tones of a wealthy, well-bred southerner. Stern made the mistake of thinking Mark to be no more than a fancy dressed kid. Now he felt a bicep which in size and hardness exceeded his own. Only he noticed it too late to stop his words.

"Listen!" he began, as he reached for Mark's arm. "We're wanting Tune—"

"Just take your cotton-picking hand off my arm."

From her vantage point on the buckskin, Calamity looked expectantly as she heard Mark's soft drawled reply. The last time she heard him speak in such a manner there followed a brawl she would never forget in which two U.S. cavalrymen were taken off with broken jaws. So she knew the danger signs.

Unfortunately for him, Stern did not.

Releasing the arm, Stern drew back his fist and threw a punch. He had something of a reputation around town as a fighting man of the first water. Against that same reputation most folks around the town felt under a disadvantage from the start.

Only Mark did not live in Tennyson, had never heard of Stern's reputation and most likely would not have been impressed by it if he had heard. All he knew was that this loud mouth wanted a fight, which same Mark sure don't aim backing away from.

Mark's left hand rose fast, deflecting the blow over his shoulder, then his right fist shot out. To the amazement of the watching crowd – and even more to the amazement of Stern – the blacksmith caught a punch with enough power to propel him backwards and knock him from his feet.

After reeling back a few steps, and causing a rapid scattering of the crowd, Stern lit down on his seat in the dust. He shook his head dazedly, then came up fast. Being trained in the old toe-to-toe bare-knuckle boxing school, Stern took a dim view of a man who avoided a blow, then hit back. With a roar like a starving and enraged grizzly, Stern charged at Mark with his fists flying.

He hit nothing but air, for Mark learned his fighting skill in a different, but much more effective school. At the last instant Mark weaved aside and clipped Stern's jaw, snapping his head back, the other hand followed and cracked the blacksmith's unlovely looking nose. Once more Stern retreated, shaking his head and wiping blood from his injured nasal organ.

"Let it drop, *hombre!*" Mark growled.

Instead of taking Mark's advice Stern came into the attack again. He took a punch in the mouth, then threw his arms around Mark's waist then clamped hold his pet hold. Mark let out a sudden grunt, for Stern had developed the crushing bear-hug hold to perfection. To get it clamped on mostly wound up with the one receiving it also collecting a couple or so broken ribs.

Mark felt the power of the crushing arms and then rammed his hands under the other man's chin. The strength in Mark's arms prevented Stern's next surging crush, holding him off just enough to prevent his obtaining full power from it. Now it became a trial of strength and Mark knew that he could hold off the other man, but wanted to get the business over with so he could go up and see his uncle. Mark remembered a trick Dusty Fog pulled once to escape from such a hold.

Raising his hands, suddenly Mark chopped down, the edges biting either side of Stern's neck even before the blacksmith could tighten his hold again. Stern let out a squawk of pain, lost his grip and took an involuntary pace to the rear.

Mark followed him up, stepping in with a fist he smashed into Stern's belly. It thudded home with a boom almost like a struck drum. Stern doubled over, legs caving under him. He did not go all the way down, for by this time Mark was riled. Up lashed Mark's other fist, catching Stern's jaw, lifting him erect, up on to his toes, then straight over on to his back. Stern landed hard, rolled over to his face, tried to push himself up. Then he went limp and collapsed to the ground and lay still.

One of the men in the crowd had long been a crony, sidekick and helper of Stern in anything the big man began. He took a look at Mark's back, forgetting the girl seated behind him, dropped his hand to his gun butt.

Calamity saw the move. Her right hand stabbed down, gripping the handle of the whip and snapping it free from the saddlehorn, she jerked her arm and the lash curled up, then shot out to crack like a rifle shot within an inch of the man's ear.

"Try it!" she warned.

The man had no such intention, being more concerned now with holding his ear and shaking his head to try and clear it of the sounds which seemed to be bouncing around inside it. He twisted around, anger plain on his face. The anger died again as he saw that Calamity still held the whip and looked capable of using it. The man gained the correct impression that had Calamity wished she could just as easily carved his ear off.

"All right, all right!" bellowed Doc Connel, walking to where Stern lay and rolling him over ungently. "You folks have had your say and seen your fun. Now for the Lord's sake let's us have some sense."

Turning towards the crowd Mark looked them over. They were the sort he expected to see present, idlers who would join any cause or follow any leader and do anything but work or wash. It would be easy to persuade such men that they represented public feeling and were acting for the best in getting Tune Counter out of Tennyson, especially when their own valuable hides might be endangered by his presence.

"One thing's for sure," drawled Mark. "Uncle Tune stays right here – unless any of you bunch want to call it different."

"In case you bunch reckon all of you agin one's good odds," Calamity put in, "I'm siding Mark, so the odds are halved. And in case any of you are wondering, they don't call me Calamity Jane for nothing."

Once again the crowd muttered, but they saw the cold gleam in Calamity's eyes and read the warning in

Mark's. So they broke up their gathering, separating into chattering groups and heading away from the doctor's home. Two of the men helped the groaning Stern to his feet and steered him towards his forge.

"You got a powerful way about you, friend," Connel remarked calmly. "Yes, sir, real powerful. So's your lady friend."

"Whooee!" Calamity whooped. "I ain't never been called a lady afore."

"There's always a first time for everything Calam," Mark replied. "Say, take my hoss down to the livery barn and give him a loose stall, will you?"

"Why, sure, right next to this here ole buckskin of mine."

"Another thing, Calam."

"Yeah?"

"Stay clear until I've seen Uncle Tune and found what he wants."

Calamity threw back her head and laughed. "For you, anything. And I do mean anything. I'll book in a room at the hotel and you can buy me a meal there."

Watching Calamity ride off Mark felt even more sure his job would not be made any easier by her presence.

"Nice gal," Connel said dryly. "Even if she does think she's Calamity Jane."

"I think she is, too," Mark answered. "And mister, I *know* Calamity Jane."

Connel threw a look after the departing girl. "Landsakes, friend, you mean that gal really is Calamity Jane?"

"Yeah. That's just who she is. Now where's Uncle Tune?"

"Up in my office. Come on up, but you can't be spending long with him."

They climbed the stairs and passed through into the small room where Connel's patients waited until he could see them. The next room had an examination couch, cupboards with medicines and other supplies and had a couple of limp white coats hanging behind the door. Connel led Mark into the small room at the rear of the building and waved a hand to the shape on the bed.

Tune Counter looked at his nephew and managed a grin. He lay in the bed, a sling on his left arm and bandages showing around his chest. He tried to sit up and brought an angry growled curse from Connel.

"Just stay where you are, this feller don't expect you to get up and dance with him."

"If he's like his pappy, and he looks like he is, he wouldn't want to dance with a man, though I'd sure keep your daughters locked up, Doc."

"Never been fool enough to have any," Connel grunted. "He allows to be kin to you."

"My nephew, Mark," Tune introduced. "Mark, this here's Doc Connel, best dang doctor and biggest fishing and hunting liar in the county."

Which told Mark that the doctor was an old friend of his uncle's and a man he could rely on in whatever blew wild around Tennyson. He shook hands with Connel and the doctor grinned.

"Cap'n Fog and the Ysabel Kid aren't coming along, are they?" Connel asked.

"Not unless they're needed real bad."

"Set and we'll tell you," Tune said.

It took Mark just five minutes to know that the situation was not as bad as he might have thought – it was a damned sight worse. Only that morning Hank Cousins had sent word from a Wells Fargo way station up country that he and his boys aimed to visit Tennyson in the very near future and they did not aim to come peaceable.

"What was that ruckus on downstairs?" Tune asked as Mark reached his conclusions as to the state of affairs.

"Nothing," Mark replied.

"You never could lie worth a cuss, boy."

Connel snorted. "Just a few of the town bums got all yeller bellied and wanted to ship you out to Sand City for safety – their safety. Mark talked 'em out of it though. He's got a convincing way with him. That right hand of his 'minds me of you'n."

"You say the word and I'll get in the wagon," Tune replied. "Sheriff Haydon's got every man tied up out at Sand City and—"

"And you lay easy there," Connel growled. "I reckon, from the way he handled Stern, young Mark here can hold down the town. 'Sides he could always deputize Miss Calamity Jane."

"Calam—!" Tune put in. "You brought Calamity Jane *here*, boy?"

"Not so's you'd notice it," Mark answered. "I met her on the trail and she was already headed here. Apart from shooting her hoss from under her and leaving her hawg-tied I couldn't see any way around it."

"Why's she here?" Tune growled.

"Why'd you think?"

"Madam Bulldog?"

"Sure," drawled Mark. "I could try and get Calam out of town."

"Would it work?"

Connel looked from uncle to nephew and suddenly the light dawned. He cut in before Mark could reply to Tune's question.

"You mean Calamity Jane's here to tangle with Madam Bulldog?"

"Why sure," Mark agreed.

"Whew!" Connel let out his breath in a gasp, then went on, "It'd be a sight to see, only Madam Bulldog's got trouble of her own. She's the one who cut Breck Cousins down."

Weakly Tune forced himself up on one elbow and gripped Mark's arm. He pointed to the town marshal's badge which lay beside his fully loaded and capped Army Colt on the chair close to the bed.

"Never had no call to take on a deputy, boy," he said. "You take this badge to the bank and ask Hoscroft, the owner, to swear you in. He's the mayor as well so he can do it. You'll maybe find him a mite pompous, boy, he acts that way. But you can reckon on him all the way should Cousins come."

A flat grin creased Mark's face. "He'll come all right. You know he will."

"All right, that's enough talk for now," growled Connel, in a tone which warned Tune he would allow no objections. "I'll go along with Mark, down to the bank, just in case any other damned fool wants to run you out of town."

"See you, then, Uncle Tune," drawled Mark, taking up his hat and settling it at the right jack-deuce angle over his off eye.

"I'm not going any place, boy," Tune replied.

At the bank Mark found Hoscroft to be affable, friendly and grimly determined to back the law to the hilt. He raised no objections and willingly swore Mark in as temporary town marshal. Nor did his help end with just swearing Mark in. He clearly did not aim to just sit back and allow Mark to face the Cousins gang alone. Opening his desk drawer Hoscroft took out a large map and spread it out before Mark. He tapped his forefinger on a point some distance from the town of Tennyson.

"This's the way station from which Cousin sent his message," he told Mark and Connel. "I had the map out and checked on things when I heard of the message. Way I see it the station's a good two days' hard ride from here."

Mark studied the map and nodded his agreement. "Even if he started off as soon as he saw the telegraph operator sending the message it'd be two days. I can't see him getting here before noon tomorrow at the earliest."

"That's the way I see it too," agreed the banker.

"They'd be lucky and need good horses to make it that early."

"Couldn't you get help from the OD Connected in time, Mark?" asked Connel, thinking of all he had heard of the murderous ways of the Cousins family.

"Not a chance of it," Mark answered. "It took me near to four days to come."

"It appears we stand or fall alone then!" boomed Hoscroft. "There are some of us, quite a few, on whom you can rely, Mark. We'll back you to the hilt."

"And there's some who might go the other way when Cousins comes," warned Connel. "That bunch you had fuss with when you arrived, Mark, some of them wouldn't be any too steady behind us when the shooting starts."

"You mean like that big feller I had fuss with?"

"Naw!" snorted Connel. "Stern's not got sense enough to pack sand into a rat-hole, but he's honest. Just hawg-stupid enough to let the bunch with him, some of 'em at any rate, talk him into thinking he was acting best for the town. Stern'd be the last one to want Tune out of town, happen he'd stopped to think it might kill Tune doing it. I reckon he was even convinced that it'd be best for Tune."

Hoscroft nodded his agreement to the words. He had seen something of the meeting, guessed at its cause and was about to go along to lend his moral support to Connel when Mark's intervention rendered the support-lending unnecessary.

"Tune ran the town with a tight, but fair, hand," he stated. "With the backing of most of the people. However, as you may know, Madam Bulldog's presence brings in much extra trade. Other people wanted to cash in on that trade – and I mean cash in. But Tune stopped it. There are some who wouldn't mind seeing him out of town and a more amenable man in his place."

"Madam Bulldog be one of them?" Mark inquired.

"Certainly not. She runs her place fairly!" barked Hoscroft. "And as I say, she put lead into Breck Cousins, so she'll be one on their visiting list when they get here."

"Reckon I'd best go and see her then," drawled Mark.

"Sure," agreed the banker. "But she'll be the least of your worries."

A grin came to Mark's lips. He thought of Calamity Jane's proposed meeting with Madam Bulldog and doubted if Hoscroft's prophecy would prove to be right. As town marshal even on a temporary basis, his responsibility was to keep peace in the town. Happen all he had heard about Madam Bulldog should be true, then when she and Calamity met the town's peace looked likely to be disturbed.

After a few more minutes of talk, receiving promises of aid, Mark left the bank. Connel had to return to his place of business and so Mark walked alone to the hotel. He saw the citizens of Tennyson showed some considerable interest in him as he passed. People peered through their windows, or out of doors as he passed. The loafers on the sidewalk also looked him over with interest, nodding towards the town marshal's badge he wore and muttering among themselves, but none offered to try and halt him or speak with him. They clearly did not aim to show their hand one way or another until he proved that he could take his fair share in the defence of the town.

He called in at the hotel's stables and found Calamity had attended to his big stallion as well as her own horse. She appeared to have taken his saddle along with her, for he could not see it on the burro by the wall.

Mark went to the hotel and saw the clerk who gave him the key to his uncle's room, for Mark intended to use it during his stay in town. He had barely entered when a knock came and he faced the door, his right hand Colt drawn and cocked ready for use.

"It's me, Mark," called Calamity's voice.

Holstering his Colt again, Mark opened the door and admitted the girl. She carried his saddle in her right hand, putting it carefully on its side in the corner of the room, then looked at him with a cheery grin.

"See you took on as marshal," she drawled. "How'd it go?"

"Uncle Tune's all right. You know what's happened here?"

"Some. I never yet saw a livery barn owner who wouldn't talk the hind leg off a dead hoss. He told me about everything that's happened here since they took the town from the gophers."

"Way I see it the Cousins bunch'll be in either late tomorrow or the next day, noon tomorrow at the earliest though," Mark told her.

"I'll side you when they come," she promised. "Anyways, I'll have tended to Madam Bulldog's needings by then."

"I was going to see you about that, Calam," Mark said. "Are you set on meeting Madam Bulldog?"

"Set as I could be," she answered. "Hell, Mark, I've been working like a dawg for nigh on six months freighting to the army. A gal's got to relax and have fun sometimes, don't she?"

Mark shrugged, seeing there would be no way of dissuading Calam from her proposed course. Short of tossing Calamity into jail, or running her out of town on a rail, he could see no way of avoiding the clash between the two women, unless, which he now doubted, Madam Bulldog should prove to be greatly over-rated. He might have asked Calamity on the strength of old friendships and did not doubt she would do as he asked, but he had never been one for using friendship to turn another from a thing they wanted to do. So he decided to sit back and allow things to fall the way the fates dealt them.

"Don't you worry none, Mark boy," said Calamity.

"After I showed her a thing or two tonight she'll know who's the better woman and that'll have you 'n' me free to hand the Cousins bunch their needings."

With that promise she headed for the door and left Mark alone with his thoughts. He cleaned his guns, made sure they were ready for use, then lay on the bed fully dressed, to catch a short rest. Something told him that he was going to need it.

The sun had just gone down when Mark entered the Bull's Head Saloon. He saw a fair crowd in attendance and wondered if this was the ordinary way of the place or if word of Calamity's arrival and intentions had gone out, bringing extra folks in to see the clash.

Mark walked across the room, ignoring the glances directed at him and the badge he wore. Knowing these small western towns he did not doubt that everyone knew he was Tune Counter's nephew, *the* Mark Counter who rode with Dusty Fog and the Ysabel Kid. Doubtless any number of them would also be speculating when Dusty and the Kid were due to arrive.

He studied the girls as he crossed the room, wanting to form his own opinion of Madam Bulldog. However, he doubted if the great lady be present. All he could see looked like run-of-the-mill dancehall girls of the kind one met in every town from Texas to California and back the long way. Not one of them appeared to be the kind to make legends or attract much attention to themselves.

Reaching the bar, Mark looked at the bartender who came towards him. The man grinned a welcome which, if Mark was any judge of such matters, looked sincere enough.

"Howdy marshal," the bartender greeted. "What'll it be?"

"Beer. Take one for yourself."

"This'n's on the house," Sam replied. "I saw you up in Quiet Town, didn't I?"

"I was there," agreed Mark.

"The name's Sam, marshal. I'm Madam Bulldog's house boss."

Mark took the drink offered to him and nodded his thanks. "Reckon you know I'm Mark Counter," he said, "Tune's nephew." He glanced around the room while Sam leaned by him clearly aiming to talk and leave his assistant to deal with the lesser clientele. "Madam Bulldog here?"

"Not just yet. Be down soon."

Although he talked with the bartender, Mark did not relax. His eyes flickered at the bar mirror, studying the room behind him. This was partly caution and partly training, for he knew better than take foolish chances in a town which contained enemies.

Three men in particular caught Mark's eye. He stayed facing Sam, but watched them in the long mirror's reflection. Two of them had been members of the crowd who wished to run his uncle out of town, which accounted for why Mark spotted them. They most certainly did not work cattle for a living, nor, despite their town suits, did they give the impression that they owned or worked in any business house of the town. To Mark, with a long experience of their kind gained in his travels and time as a law officer, they spelled cheap tinhorn card shark, goldbrick salesmen, or petty thief.

The third man was none of these things – he was much more dangerous. He wore somewhat expensive and dandy range clothes, a thing Mark could hardly hold against him. His face bore a tan, yet he did not strike Mark as being a cowhand. Comparing him with the other two Mark decided he could not be very tall. Yet he had a faintly hidden truculence about him that did not go with his lack of inches. Mark knew the signs, could read them well. This small man had all the markings of a real fast proddy hard-case, which, viewing his lack of inches, meant he relied on gun speed, not muscle, to get him by.

Unless Mark was mistaken, the trio appeared to be giving him much more than casual attention. They watched him enter, cross to the bar and stand at it. Then they thrust their heads together and talked. From the repeated looks they threw his way, Mark guessed himself to be the subject of their conversation.

"Sam," Mark said quietly. "Who're those three citizens sitting there to the right of the vingt-un layout?"

To give him credit, Sam did not stare directly at the men. He clearly had learned his trade in the saloons which gave support to the law, for he merely glanced around the room with keen, all seeing gaze, not pausing his look on the three men. For all that he answered Mark's question as soon as his quick look around ended.

"The two townies are Wardle and Schanz. Never seen the other, except his type and we've both seen *that*. Them two come here to try and open a saloon, when the town broke open after Madam arrived. Only they didn't have enough money and the bank wouldn't loan any. So they came here, wanted to set up a game and cut Madam in on the profits. She wouldn't have any of it."

"What do they do around town?"

"Play here some nights, join the cowhand games."

"Play straight?"

"We never caught them at anything crooked," Sam replied. "And Madam keeps her eyes on them. We run a straight place and that's the way she aims to keep it."

"Then they don't make much here?" asked Mark, watching the men, seeing the small hard-case rise, seeing for the first time that he wore two guns.

"Enough. You know how it is, their kind can lick the pants off most cowhands, even in a straight game," Sam answered. "I heard they run another game in their room at the hotel. It's only a rumor though. Nobody talks much about it."

By this time the short man had reached the bar,

halting to Mark's left and a short way along. Mark felt his back hair rise stiff and bristly, the instinct of years of wearing guns warning him of danger.

"Hey, bardog!"

Although the term "bardog" had much use throughout the west it had never been considered polite to use it to a bartender's face, or when calling for service; the small man did so. Sam scowled, seeing the man's attention directed straight at him. So Sam ignored the small man and waited to be asked in a more polite manner.

"Serve you, friend?" asked the second bartender moving up as Sam turned to talk with Mark once more.

"I want him," replied the small man, pointing to Sam.

"He's busy."

Turning to face the second bartender fully, the small man's face twisted into an ugly snarl.

"He's the boss bartender and Al Cordby don't take no dealing with underlings. So get out of the way."

Sam threw a look pregnant with meaning to Mark, seeing that the name had not gone unnoticed by the big Texan. Over the past couple of years Al Cordby had built something of a name for himself in Texas. Folks spoke of him as a fast gun hired killer. Mean as hell and a hater of any man taller than himself.

This was the man who stood along the bar from Mark. He had come up to the bar for a purpose and that purpose was not just to buy a drink.

Slapping his right hand hard on the bar top, Cordby looked hard at Sam.

"I want you to serve me, bardog."

"He's serving me."

Mark spoke quietly. Yet in some way his words reached out around the room. The piano player hit a jangling discord and stopped playing, talk died down, every eye went to the bar, and those nearest to it set down their glasses ready to dive for cover.

For a long moment Cordby studied Mark. He had the

true killer attitude, the calm, detached, confident way which served to disturb and scare lesser men when faced by a known fast gun. Cordby made no move. His right hand stayed where it lay on the bar, but the left hand hung hidden by his body. He studied Mark, noting the way the big Texan's guns hung, knowing that here stood a man who wore the rig of one who could draw real fast. That increased Cordby's hate, strengthened his intention of carrying out the work for which he had been hired.

"I want him here, big man!" he said.

"Now you know what it is to want," Mark replied.

Still Cordby did not turn to face Mark, just twisted his head and looked. A cold, savage snarl came to his lips.

"Big man, huh?" he asked. "You're the big man who aims to stop Hank Cousins and his boys coming in here and roughing the town up?"

"That's what they tell me," Mark replied.

"You're setting all these folks up for trouble they could avoid," Cordby went on, seeing the crowd hung on his words. "You're aiming to keep Tune Counter here instead of sending him to Sand City where he'll be safe."

"That's just what I'm going to do," Mark replied.

"And you reckon you're big enough man to do it?"

"I reckon I'm big enough to do it."

"Big men, huh?" Cordby sneered.

"Depends," replied Mark.

"What on?"

"How big a man I'm talking to. There's some around who likely reckon I'm a midget."

Nothing Mark might have said could have raised Cordby's hate against him more. Cordby felt all too fully his lack of inches and resented any man making even a casual reference to them.

For his part Mark saw the clash coming. He knew Cordby came to the bar with the intention of picking a fight with him and could guess at the reason. The two men sat at their table and watched everything with interest. Only one person in the room moved. A tall, blonde girl went upstairs at a fast walk and disappeared from sight at the top, likely headed away from danger, Mark thought.

"Get me another beer, Sam," Mark said, taking his eyes from Cordby for an instant, then watching him again.

"Leave it!" the words cracked from Cordby's lips. "Listen good to me, big man. You get out of this town and take your kin with you. That way Hank Cousins and his boys'll be satisfied."

"Will, huh?"

"Sure they will."

Now Cordby was not speaking to Mark, but directing his words to the crowd. Some of them even looked as if they might believe him. Mark now knew why Cordby came to the bar. To force the issue, to either make Mark back-water in which case he would be finished as town marshal, for none would follow his lead, or to terminate Mark's period in office by means of a bullet. Either way he would give strength to the men who hired him, allow them to dominate their will upon the town. The fate of Tennyson City hung in the balance.

All this Mark knew. If he faced the challenge he would bring the town around behind his back. If he failed to handle Cordby, or if he backed down, his Uncle Tune would be on the wagon and headed for Sand City before an hour passed and most likely Madam Bulldog would be run out of town at the same time.

"I said get me another beer, Sam," Mark drawled.

Against the flat defiance Cordby prepared to make his move. He knew Mark could not see his left hand, knew also that most men tended to ignore the left hand as a faction in a gunfight. There were a few men who could draw and shoot equally well with either hand, but they could almost be numbered on the fingers of a man's two hands. Most men, even men who wore two guns all the time, kept the left hand weapon in reserve, to have another six shots ready instantly in case of urgent need.

Cordby pivoted around fast, his left hand stabbing to his side, dipping, closing on the butt of his gun, and bringing it forth even as he made his turn. Yet before he faced Mark fully, Cordby knew he had called the play wrong.

The significance of the hidden left hand did not escape Mark, for he knew men who handled their guns with ambidextrous skill. So he stood ready for just such a move as Cordby now made.

His right hand dipped, fingers closing about the ivory butt of the Colt in his right side holster, thumb curling around and drawing back the hammer even as he lifted the gun from leather. In slightly over half a second, even as Cordby faced him, and before the man's gun could line, Mark's gun came clear and roared.

For an instant the short killer's face showed amazement, horror almost, as he realized his favorite play had failed him at last. Then Mark's Army Colt roared, the recoil kicked the barrel up and a .44 bullet ripped into Cordby's head, threw him backwards to crash to the sawdust covered floor, dead.

There had been no time to shoot in any other way. Cordby's intention had been to kill Mark and the big Texan acted the only way he dare, by killing Cordby first.

Across the room Cordby's two pards came to their feet. Wardle thrust his hand under his coat to where a short barrelled Colt hung in a shoulder clip. A shot spat out, a lighter crack than the roar of an Army Colt. It sounded from the stairs and splinters erupted from the table between Wardle and Schanz. Looking towards the shooter, Wardle froze, letting his hand stay under the coat but not trying to draw his gun. He saw who had cut in and knew Madam Bulldog's bullet hit the table because that was where she intended it to go.

Mark turned fast, his gun slanting towards the stairs for an instant, then swung back towards the two men as the crowd scattered from them. He watched Wardle's hand come clear of the coat, then turned his eyes once more to the two women on the stairs. One was the blonde who he had seen going up and thought had been headed for safety, only Mark knew he had miscalled her intentions, for she went to fetch help. The other woman clearly must be Madam Bulldog. Looking at her, Mark studied for an instant the Colt Cloverleaf she held. Then he nodded, this surely was Madam Bulldog and she looked like she might live up to her reputation.

However, there would be time to get to know her better when a small matter had been attended to. He nodded towards the woman as she stood watching him, her gun still in her hand.

"Thank you kindly, ma'am," he said.

The big Colt spun on his finger and dropped back into the holster. He started across the room with long, purposeful strides. The two men watched his coming and moved around to try and keep the table between themselves and the advancing Texan.

Madam Bulldog gave Viola her Cloverleaf and told the blonde to take it to her room. She watched Mark crossing the room, then waved two of the waiters, pointing to Cordby's body. The men knew what they must do and went forward, the town undertaker with them. Before they removed the dead man they stopped to see how Mark handled the other two.

Neither Wardle nor Schanz were brave men. Given a drunk in a side-alley they could handle him with ease. Faced with a big, sober and very angry man their courage oozed out of them. Nor did either have the slightest intention of trying to draw the guns they

carried. They had seen Cordby die before the fast drawn
Army Colt and knew Mark could handle them both in
the matter of gun-play.

Shoving the table aside, Mark reached out a big right
hand. He gripped the front of Wardle's jacket and shirt,
bunching them up as he dragged the man towards him.
A look of relief came to Schanz's face, but did not stay
there for long, for Mark wiped it off with a backhand
slap which spun the man around, sent him staggering
into the wall. In a continuance of the same move Mark
brought his arm around and landed a bare-hand slap
across Wardle's face, snapping his head back and spinning him the other way.

Coldly Mark looked at the two men. "You pair tried
to set me up for a kill," he said quietly, yet grimly.

"You – you got us wrong!" Wardle croaked, wiping
a tricle of blood from the corner of his mouth. "We
didn't know what Cordby aimed to do."

Mark's grin looked colder than ice as he replied,
"You're a liar."

The correct answer to such a statement should have
been a fast drawn Colt, for the word "liar" was regarded
as one of the supreme insults in the west. Yet the man at
whom Mark directed it made no reply. He made his feet
and stood staring at the big Texan. Schanz also stood
up, his eyes showed hate, but they showed fear too.

"Tune Counter's staying in town," Mark went on.
"And if Cousins wants him he'll have to go through me
first. But you pair won't be here to see it. If you're in
town tomorrow at dawn I'll shoot you on sight."

"You—!" began Schanz, meaning to stand on his
Constitutional rights.

He saw the look on Mark's face and discarded his
rights. Turning on his heel he made a rapid dive for the
batwing doors of the saloon, beating Wardle to them by
a scant half second.

For a moment Mark stood watching the doors, he
heard the footsteps fading away along the sidewalk and

knew the two men would not be back. Their kind would never face a determined man and they would not dare go against him, not face to face. From behind they might be a danger, but he doubted if they would be in Tennyson when he made his morning rounds.

"I've seen to having Cordby removed."

Mark turned at the words and found Madam Bulldog standing nearby. He looked her over with some interest and knew that here stood a woman who might even be able to outdo Calamity Jane in the matters at which they both claimed pre-eminence.

He threw a glance towards the bar where the local undertaker and the waiters, seeing there would be no further developments, lifted the body and carried it towards the rear door.

"Thanks, ma'am," he replied.

"Are all you Counter men tall?" she inquired, studying his six foot three inches of height and the great spread of his shoulders.

"Most of us," Mark grinned. "My Uncle Shorty though, he's only six foot tall. We don't talk about him much."

A laugh changed Madam Bulldog's face, made it look pleasant, friendly and attractive. She lost the smile after a moment.

"Those two set Cordby on to you?" she asked.

"Why sure," agreed Mark.

"Saw it all. I thought Tune was fast with a gun, but you're faster."

"You'll be making me blush next, ma'am."

"The day *you* blush will be a day to remember," she sniffed. "Tell you one thing though. You've got the town now."

Mark knew what she meant. His handling of Cordby, his proof of how fast he could draw and with what skill he could plant home his bullets, had not gone without notice amongst the customers. They knew they had a good man with a gun wearing the law badge and would be the more willing to follow his lead when the time came.

"Those pair, ma'am," Mark said, "you reckon they're working with Cousins?"

"No. They saw a chance of getting Tune out of town – and knowing he would be unlikely to come back, so they took it."

"Huh, huh!" grunted Mark. "Anybody in town likely to side with Cousins and his bunch when they come."

She grinned. It was a hard, cold grin, without humor. "Not since you cut Al Cordby down."

At that moment Madam Bulldog stopped looking and talking to Mark and stepped by him, making for the door. Mark turned and almost groaned aloud as he saw the reason for Madam Bulldog's departure.

Calamity Jane entered the Bull's Head Saloon, shoving through the batwing door as she had done in innumerable places and towns throughout the west. She left behind her the world of the good ladies of a town, entering the protected domain of the dancehall girl. This time Calam took a bare three steps into the room before she found her way blocked, a woman standing full in her path.

"The door's there, girlie," said Madam Bulldog, indicating the entrance through which Calamity came into the room.

"Yeah!" replied Calamity, studying the woman she had ridden almost five hundred miles to meet. Then, although she could make a real accurate guess at the answer, went on: "Who're you?"

Hands on hips, feet braced apart, stood Madam Bulldog. She read the challenge in Calamity's eyes and knew that here stood no ordinary saloongirl trying to impress folks with how tough she was. To the saloonkeeper's way of seeing, Calamity formed a definite and dangerous menace, more so than the average tough calico cat who came to try Madam Bulldog out and left a sadder, pain-filled and wiser woman. The red-haired girl, for all her fancy, man's clothes, would need different handling than the normal run of challengers.

"I'm Madam Bulldog – and who might *you* be?"

Calamity grinned broadly. "I might be Belle Starr, or Poker Alice, or Madame Moustache, but I'm none of them. I'm Calamity Jane."

A matter of interest, anticipation and excitement rose from the watching and listening crowd, for all had heard of Calamity Jane, and all could guess at why she came to Tennyson.

So could Madam Bulldog and in that moment, she felt grateful to Calamity for making the pilgrimage. Madam Bulldog could see that all thoughts of danger, all fears of the Cousins' gang, already weakened by Mark's prompt action in dealing with Wardle and Cordby, now became forgotten in the anticipation of the forthcoming clash between herself and Calamity Jane. So, although she did not wish for the clash, Madam Bulldog did not side-step it either.

"Calamity Jane, huh?" said Madam Bulldog with a sniff which might have meant anything or nothing.

Everybody in the room waited and watched. They wondered if Calamity would land on the other woman with tooth and claw, in a brawl which would make a legend, or if the girl aimed to make her play with guns, which would also be memorable if not as lasting or entertaining.

Calamity herself had the same thoughts. She took in the hard rubbery way in which the other woman stood, noted the powerful looking arms and general air of tough capability.

"Yes, sir," thought Calamity, "this gal's worth riding to see."

She thought also that such a meeting might not be terminated too quickly by licking Madam Bulldog physically. First Madam had to learn that her other talents high though they might be, stood second to Calamity Jane's. With that in mind Calamity held off her physical attack until she had showed Madam how a real wild and woolly gal could cuss.

"You know what I reckon you are?" Calamity asked. "I reckon you're a—"

There followed a string of profanity good enough to turn a thirty year army sergeant green with envy as Calamity poured her vilification on to the other woman's head in a fast flow.

After almost three minutes Calamity stopped, sure she had rocked Madam Bulldog to the toes of her dainty high heeled shoes. Only Madam gave no sign of being either rocked or shocked. Instead she came back with and proceeded to heap on the girl a flow of cursing of equal length, pungency and power of abuse.

For once in her life Calamity looked surprised and taken aback. She grudgingly admitted that Madam Bulldog could pour on the abuse real fast, hard and colorful.

At the end of Madam's flow, she turned and walked back to the bar with Calamity on her heels Mark Counter watched them go, then followed to take up his beer. He grinned as he looked around the silent and still room where the crowd, customers and workers alike, sat in rapt attention. Calamity started cursing once more and a man holding an aces full house, with over two hundred dollars of his money already in the pot, sat staring, ignoring the game. At the faro layout the bets lay forgotten. The wheel of fortune came to a halt but the lucky winners did not trouble to gather in their winnings for they stared and listened like men turned to stone.

The rules for a cursing match had long been known throughout the west. Now Calamity Jane tangled in such a match with Madam Bulldog. The girl had learned her business from the inspired utterances of miners, soldiers and bullwhackers. To this she brought and added all her native powers to improve and increase her vocabulary. Yet for all of that she gained the idea that Madam Bulldog commanded just as good a flow.

They matched each other word for word, invoked weird and horrible gods, suggested each other had unmentionable diseases, accused each other of every low act the human body could possibly perform and several for which it would be impossible for any human body to perform. They cursed each other's ancestors, descendants and distant kin. Sweat came to their faces, running down their cheeks. Calamity tore her bandana off and Madam Bulldog's hair came down, hanging around her face while her make-up became streaked and then washed away.

Not a sound came from the room. Every man present would have given all he owned to have those inspired utterings written down so he might read and learn from them.

Then slowly Calamity's voice trailed off. She looked glassy eyed and dazed under the strain. No longer would her mind function and her mouth felt dry, her tongue unable to force another word through her lips.

With a croak of frustrated rage Calamity swung her hand around, fist clenched for a blow and in doing so she admitted her defeat at the cussing match. Only the blow did not land. Mark Counter, watching and listening with the same rapt attention as the others, saw the start of the move and took steps to prevent it. He moved forward and his big hand shot out to catch her arm, holding it before the fist touched Madam Bulldog's face.

"You're licked, Calam," he said quietly.

The girl nodded her agreement, clinging to the bar and unable to make a single sound in reply. She stared through glassy eyes as Madam Bulldog spat out another flow of curses, driving home the point that Calamity Jane had been out-cussed, over-cussed and cussed plumb into the ground. Although her throat felt raw and she could hardly think or breathe, Madam Bulldog made her final speech. She knew Calamity to be licked at cussing, but doubted if the girl would be willing to let things go with just that.

So Madam Bulldog turned to face the bar, looking at the state of her face and barely holding down a gasp of horror. She nodded to Sam, not wishing to speak and knowing he would understand her needs. Sam did, he poured out a couple of schooners of beer, a drink which at other times Madam would not have thought of touching, but which he knew would be the only thing she could manage at the moment. Placing a schooner before each woman, Sam stepped back, grinning broadly.

Calamity took up the glass and drank deeply, watching Madam Bulldog in the mirror, trying to carry on drinking after the woman finished. However, Madam saw the way Calamity looked and so tilted back the big schooner. Calamity managed three-quarters of her glass before lack of breath caused her to put it down, she watched Madam empty her's and knew the task ahead would be far harder than she at first imagined.

"It's not so easy, is it, Calam?" asked Mark Counter as he watched Madam make for her room to tidy her appearance before attending to her customers.

"It sure ain't," Calamity replied, mopping her face with the bandana, all the beauty treatment she needed. "This gal's going to take some licking."

Half an hour passed before Madam Bulldog returned to the barroom with her face once more made-up ready for business and her hair tidy again. She crossed straight to the bar, making for Calamity and the crowd looked on, wondering at what the two women would clash next. The air of eager expectancy had not diminished after seeing Calamity out-cussed, for all knew she was not the kind of girl to take defeat lying down. Most of the crowd hoped for a fight, but once more they did not get their wish for Calamity grinned and said:

"They reckon you play poker, Madam."

In this Calamity showed wisdom. Not that she feared a physical tangle with the other woman. At any other time she would have been only too willing to pitch into Madam Bulldog tooth and claw, but she knew it would not be an easy matter to whip the saloonkeeper and wanted to keep out of the fight until after she helped Mark Counter meet the Cousins gang, if possible. Madam Bulldog's motives were the same. She also wanted to be unimpaired by the injuries a fight with Calamity must bring, so that when Cousins and his bunch came she could lend Mark a hand and save her own life, for she knew Cousins would be after her as well as Tune Counter.

"I do," she replied to Calamity's suggestion. "Do you?"

"Let's set, deal a few 'n' find out, shall we?"

Madam nodded, then looked towards the bar. "Sam, a new, unopened deck of cards. That table in front of the bar suit you, Calamity?"

"Why, sure."

For a long moment Madam Bulldog studied the girl, almost as if she felt she ought to recognize, or at least know, Calamity from somewhere. Sure she had heard of Calamity Jane, there were few in the west who had not. Yet few, a very few indeed, knew Calamity's full name of Martha Jane Canary, for it never received mention when folks talked about her. Madam Bulldog knew her only as Calamity Jane and after the long look shook her head, clearing the thoughts of recognition from it. She led the way to the table and they took their seats facing each other.

"Mark!" Madam called. "Bring a box of chips, and come on over to act as look out for us."

"I'll do just that," Mark replied, taking a new deck of cards and box of poker chips from Sam, then crossing to join the two women at the table.

Once more the other entertainments of the evening

lapsed and became forgotten as a crowd gathered around the table, standing in a circle to see the sport. They all knew Madam Bulldog's skill, but also had heard of Calamity's poker playing prowess and so expected a good display. Certainly Calamity would be on her mettle after losing out on the cussing match.

Calamity took the deck of cards, turning it between her fingers, seeing the box carried the mark of a well known firm of card makers and that the Federal tax seal remained intact. This meant little, as she knew well, for crooked gambling supply houses could easily steam off the seal, doctor the cards and reseal it again so as to defy detection. With this thought in mind she broke the seal, took out the cards and flipped the jokers aside.

"When I play," she stated, "there's no limit, no wild cards, and no ladies in the game."

"I play any way the others want," answered Madam and Calamity's annoyed grunt told her she had scored the point with her words.

She sat back and without annoyance watched Calamity give the cards a quick but thorough check to ensure they had not been marked or, by having the others filed down a minute piece at the edge, certain cards being larger than the remainder of the deck so as to allow them to be located and used during the game. Madam took no offence at the precautions, for they gave her an insight into Calamity's knowledge of the game and left her sure of one thing, Calamity knew more than a little about the art of playing card games for money.

Calamity gave a sweeping glance round the table, making sure that nothing lay on it which might contain a tiny mirror to show Madam the value of the cards as she dealt them. Nor did Madam have either a small bandage on a finger and concealing all but the tip of a thumb-tack, or a ring which might carry a tiny sharp spike either of which could be used for 'pegging'; marking the cards during play by pricking the backs in certain spots to show their value. This was an old crooked gambling method, but one which still brought in profit when playing against the unwary.

Although Madam's hands carried neither bandage nor rings, Calamity knew there were many other ways by which the deck might be marked during play. Nailing, pressing the thumbnail into the edge of the cards, making a tiny mark, dangerous against an alert opponent, but used in some circles. Waving, bending the desired cards slightly, again risky when the other player or players knew anything about their business. Daubing, this offered less chance of detection on the cards, but carried the risk of the opposition seeing the small, concealed spot of dye of slightly lighter or darker hue than the back of the deck, or spotting the tell-tale stain on the thumb or finger used to transfer the dye to the cards.

All these methods Calamity knew of and although she took precautions against them and aimed to keep her eyes open for any kind of crooked play, some instinct told her she did not need to worry, the game would be fair.

She gave the cards a rapid riffle-stack, then thrust them across the table to Madam Bulldog who took them up and also riffled them. Madam laid the cards on the table top and nodded to the girl.

"Cut," Madam said. "Draw or stud?"

"Make it dealer's choice," Calamity said. "Cut light, lose all night."

Giving out with the old poker adage Calamity cut deep into the deck and left the completion of the cut to her opponent, watching for any sign that Madam aimed to lay the cards in the same order as before the cut. Madam took up the cards and, deciding to make the first game draw poker, flipped five cards face down to each of them.

So began a card game which would go down amongst the legends of the west. A game of skill, science and bluff which would have made many an acknowledged master of poker look to his laurels.

From the very first hand Mark, no novice at the poker game himself, saw that it would be a hard fought contest. Both women had an extensive knowledge of the game, both its mathematics and, although neither of them had ever heard the word, of its psychology. The early hands saw them playing an almost classic game and in such case, their skill being near enough equal, neither could make any impression on the other's pile of chips.

However, Mark got the idea that of the two Madam Bulldog showed the better poker sense. Calamity's volatile nature led her to pile on the pressure when the cards started falling her way. For a time the cards ran Calamity's way and it seemed that she could do no wrong. At draw she would take one card to two pairs and a third member of one of her pairs would pop up like a trained pig, or she would go for one to an inside straight (which was never good poker) and that required one arrived as if drawn by a magnet.

Against such luck no amount of skill could prevail and even though she played every hand in a manner which would have brought a nod of approval from Hoyle: always working on the widely accepted, but erroneous belief, that Hoyle had played and mastered the game of poker; Madam Bulldog lost heavily. The crowd watched everything, guessing, or trying to guess what each woman held. They groaned their sympathy when Madam lost on a good hand which Calamity's lucky draw, or lucky arrival of a last up-card winner, snatched from her.

At the end of two hours' play Calamity stood almost fifteen thousand dollars ahead and Sam, who knew his boss' business, felt panic, for he watched the way the girl bet. Madam could not stand much more of this kind of loss.

For her part Calamity enjoyed every minute of the game; so did Madam Bulldog, even though losing for, if she could hang on long enough, she knew the cards must change their ways.

"Aw, hell," drawled Calamity, hauling in a pot. "Whyn't we move to a bigger table. I've hardly got room to move an elbow for my winnings."

Mark grinned and Madam Bulldog's face showed an expression at this ancient poker artifice. She sat back, with no sign of worry, or interest in the growing pile before Calamity.

"Deal," she said.

"Damned if I don't buy into a freight outfit with my winnings," Calamity went on, scooping up the cards and riffling them. "Wouldn't want to keep this place going though, never could stand being in one place. Sorry I can't stack 'em better than this, Madam, got so much loot in front of me. Say, Mark, did I ever tell you about the time I took a five thousand dollar pot with three threes?"

For her part Madam ignored the words, playing each hand on its merit, neither being scared out of playing a good hand because the luck went against her, nor trying to make Calamity look small on taking her on an understrength hand. The taunt that Calamity intended to win her place just rolled off her back and she waited.

Then:

"Aces full," Calamity said in a bored tone, as if drawing a full house of three Aces and two nines had become such a regular thing as to bore her. "You had me worried. I thought you'd filled those fours you were after."

"That's funny," replied Madam Bulldog calmly. "I *did* get them."

She turned her cards face up and Calamity stared at four threes and a four. It came as a real shock to Calamity who had been betting high, wide and handsome, assuming that Madam Bulldog drew a flush which her hand would beat.

Thinking of the game later Mark decided the earlier

run of luck clouded Calamity's judgment. There had been turns when she had pulled a last card miracle at stud during those earlier hands. Then, as almost always happens, the cards swung their favor the other way completely. From being able to do everything right Calamity made the complete circle and all went wrong.

Now Madam Bulldog started to needle Calamity in the same way the girl worked on her while winning and Calamity, while knowing she was being needled, rose to the bait like a hungry rainbow trout after a floating fly.

Having found Calamity's weaker game to be stud, Madam dealt it every time and mocked the girl for changing to draw. Against her better judgment, Calamity tossed out the first cards face down, then turned the second over to bet on instead of all five face down for draw.

The taunting and goading were all accepted as completely fair and honest tactics in the rough-and-tumble of no limit poker and a player who was not a past-master, or mistress, of the art of applying the needle, had no right to be playing.

"Oh hum!" sighed Madam Bulldog, tossing a straight flush face down on the table, into the dead-wood, acting as if she had bluffed Calamity on a seven high, no-nothing hand. "I always reckon you should have the guts to call them when you bet on them. Lucky for me you didn't though."

Calamity let out an annoyed grunt, not sure whether she could have beaten Madam's unseen hand and wishing she had paid to see. She would not sink to the depths of trying to look at the hand without paying for the privilege.

So Calamity sat back and the next time she felt Madam to be bluffing, she called the bet.

"I've what it looked like," replied Madam, contemptuously exposing a ten high flush. "You never called on that hoss-droppings you held, did you?"

The game went on. Calamity's temper crackled, but

she knew to allow it to burst would be certain proof that she had met a better poker player and worse in her eyes, would brand her as a poor loser.

At eleven o'clock Mark rose from the table, leaving the saloon to make his rounds of the town. He walked the silent streets and kept his ears and eyes open. He knew Wardle and Schanz would never have the guts to stack against him on even terms, but they might chance a shot from some dark alley. So Mark stayed alert, using the caution he gained while serving as a deputy under Dusty Fog in Quiet Town.

He gave little thought to the big game at the Bull's Head. The meeting had so far come off much more peaceably than he expected. It also had not gone the way he would have bet on it going, for so far Calamity had been licked at cussing and it looked like Madam could lick her at poker, for Mark admitted the saloonkeeper had been the better player of the two, with the wisdom of extra years to back her. That there would be a head-on physical clash Mark did not doubt, but he also doubted if it would come until Calamity lost out at drinking and cards. It might even not come off until after the Cousins bunch arrived, depending on how Calamity felt at losing.

Mark did not hurry his rounds, nor did he waste time in worrying about possible dangers. He called into the jail house, lit the lamp, checked the place, filled the desk log and left. Doc Connel's house lay in darkness and Mark doubted if the good doctor would take kindly to being wakened at this hour to answer pointless questions about Tune Counter's health.

So after almost an hour Mark returned to the Bull's Head. Passing the hotel he came on Viola carrying something he recognized as Calamity's war bag and bedroll. From the look of this, and the fact that customers streamed out of the batwing doors, Mark judged the game to be over and that Calamity had come off second best.

In the saloon the waiters harried the last of the customers through the door, driving out the indomitable few who stayed to the bitter end of the game. Madam Bulldog always insisted that the workers cleared everything up before they left at night, that all bottles and glasses be removed from the tables and all be left ready for the swampers to do their cleaning in the morning. Behind the bar Sam had the cash drawer open and counted the night's take. It was heavier than usual for the spectators of the clash spent well as they watched.

"Hi Mark!" called Calamity, taking the bedroll and war bag from Viola and looking to where the big Texan stood at the door of the saloon. "You need a deputy?"

"I thought you didn't need work, Calam gal," Mark replied.

"I do now," she answered with a grin, then turned to Madam Bulldog. "I'll change into my old gear and leave the rest in there."

After Calamity left the room Madam Bulldog sighed. "That girl's good. I would hate to play her in another ten years' time."

"She lost heavy?"

"Heavy enough. Have a beer, unless you fancy something a mite stronger."

"Beer'll do."

When Calamity stepped from the saloonkeeper's office she wore a battered cavalry kepi, an old shirt, patched old pants and worn boots. Her old walnut gripped Navy Colt stuck in her waistband and she carried all her belongings, including the new gunbelt and holster with her. However, for all of losing her fancy duds, the new gunbelt and ivory butted Colt and her buckskin horse, Calamity had not offered to wager the most important of all her belongings, her saddle, carbine, whip and hand-gun. The rest she had lost meant nothing to her. She could always work and earn money to buy new clothes and a new horse. But without a saddle she could not work and without her firearms she could not protect herself while working. The whip too was a part of her stock-in-trade and she clung to it.

"Have a drink, Calamity," Madam said as the girl handed over her belongings. "If you want broke money it's yours."

"Thanks," grinned Calamity, holding out a hand. "You play a mean hand at poker and you licked me fair and square. I'll take that drink though."

"What'll it be, Calam?" asked Sam from behind the bar.

"Whisky. You drinking with me, Madam?"

Once more Madam Bulldog read the open challenge and did not try to avoid it. She hated drinking in public and would never have a better chance than right now, to show Calamity how well she could handle a bottle.

Sam read the answer to his unasked question and poured four fingers of the house's best whisky into each woman's glass. Calamity took her's up, turned it between her fingers and looked at it.

"This is ten year old stock," Madam remarked calmly.

"It's not very big for its age, is it?" Calamity countered.

There was a raw challenge in the words which Madam met head on and without a thought of avoiding it. She waved a hand towards the two pint glasses mostly used for beer.

"Fill them up, Sam," she said.

Sam threw a startled look at his boss, but knew better than raise any objections. So he poured out the whisky, emptying one bottle and starting another to fill the glasses. He threw a look at Mark, hoping for guidance, but Mark stood back and let things go.

"You're not drinking Mark," said Madam Bulldog.

"I've had all I want for one night," he replied.

"So be it. Don't let moss grow in the glass, girlie."

Saying that, Madam Bulldog raised her glass in a cheery salute to Calamity and started to drink. Not to be outdone, Calamity also raised her glass and began to let the whisky flow down her throat. She bit down a gagging cough as the liquor hit her, for Madam calmly held her own glass and drank at it without showing a sign.

Not until the glasses were both empty did Calamity and Madam Bulldog set them down. Then they looked at each other quizzically. The whisky had not taken its effect yet and they stood erect, watching the other for any sign of weakening. On seeing none Madam nodded to Sam and ordered him to refill the glasses.

"Here's to you," said Calamity, gripping her glass by the handle and lifting it from the bar-top.

Then the whisky hit her, landing with the kick of a Missouri mule. Calamity gave a gasp, her eyes glazed over, the glass fell from her hand, her knees buckled and she went to the floor in a heap.

For a moment Madam stood swaying over the girl, then raised her own glass and took a long swallow. She set the glass on the bar, turned to Mark and said in a cold sober tone:

"Don't reckon she could take her likker after all."

And then Madam Bulldog's legs folded under her and she piled in a limp heap on to Calamity Jane.

Dawn's cold grey light crept through the window of Calamity Jane's room at the hotel. The girl lay where Mark Counter left her, for he carried her home the previous night. Apart from removing her kepi and boots Mark had not troubled to undress her, but rolled her under the blankets of the bed while she still wore her shirt and pants.

Calamity stirred, groaned, opened her eyes, clutched at her forehead and hurriedly closed her eyes again. She gave a moan, her mouth felt like she had been licking up skunk droppings and her head throbbed fit to burst. For a moment she lay on the bed, then her stomach started to turn somersaults, or so it seemed to her.

With a low moan, Calamity rolled from her bed and staggered to the door of the room, opened it and made a hurried dash down the back stairs, out into the cold chill air of the morning, racing for the backhouse and hoping she would make it in time to prevent disgracing herself.

A very sick and angry Calamity came from the backhouse. She felt mean, ornery on top of the sickness, the sort of condition when she had to have a drink, or go and bust something. So it was unfortunate that at that moment she saw the old swamper open the Bull's Head Saloon's side door ready to start his morning's cleaning.

Calamity, who had been in her present condition on several previous occasions, decided that the only sure cure would be a hair of the dog which bit her. Also she decided that her condition stemmed from the liquor at Madam Bulldog's place and it must be Madam Bulldog who served the hair. So, with that thought in her mind, she headed for the saloon.

On reaching the building she shoved open the side door and walked into the empty, almost deserted barroom. Calamity groaned a little as she looked at the bar and remembered the previous evening. She saw the glass of whisky left by Madame Bulldog, at least, it was a glass half full with whisky and would be just what she needed to satisfy her restless stomach.

The old swamper turned. He also had an eye on the whisky, for only on very rare occasions did he see such a windfall left behind. Sam would have removed the glass the previous night, but had been more than occupied in getting Madam Bulldog to bed, so it lay where she set it down on the bar top.

"Wha' you wan', gal?" asked the swamper, casting avaricious glances at the inviting glass of whisky and licking his lips. "Ain't open yet."

"You soon will be," Calamity replied and stepped forward.

"Cain't come in here!" wailed the man, stepping before her.

"Don't rile me pappy!" growled Calamity: "Or I'll ram you feet first and head deep into the wall so we can use your ears for a hatrack."

With that she pushed by him and headed for the bar. He stood staring at her, then let out a moan of annoyance as he saw the girl take up the glass and raise it to her lips. The threat did not worry him, but this drinking of what he regarded as his private property hurt his tenderest feelings. His sense of duty was outraged and his stumpy, bowed old legs headed him across the room, then upstairs where he would find people to help him attend to the matter.

Calamity held the glass in a shaking hand. The raw smell of the whisky came up to hit her, causing her to gag and her stomach to make a violent heave. She fought down the nausea with an effort, knowing that the whisky would still her troubled insides. She drank and felt a shudder run through her, then set the glass down on the bar top again. After standing for a few hours the whisky had a bitter bite to it and she felt she could use a cold beer to balance its effects.

Raising her hand Calamity banged it down hard on the bar top. The sudden noise jarred her head and she let out a moan. The whisky might have settled her stomach but it did nothing to improve her temper. The pain in her head caused her to bang again and left her voice in a yell.

"Hey! About getting this lousy joint open?"

"We're closed!" answered a sleepy but annoyed female voice from upstairs.

That did not make Calamity feel any better. She pounded on the bar top once more and repeated her yelled demand for service. A sound from the head of the stairs brought her attention to where Viola and two more girls, tousle-haired, sleep eyed, with housecoats dragged over their night wear, stood glaring down at her with hostile gaze.

"Why don't you go where you came from?" asked Viola, never at her best or most friendly when wakened from her sleep in the small hours of the morning.

"Why don't you come down and try to make me?" Calamity answered truculently.

An angry curse came from Viola's lips. She studied Calamity and weighed up her chances of a single-handed tangle with the girl, then discarded the idea as being out of the question. However, her two friends also felt riled at having their beauty sleep despoiled and ruined. Between the three of them they ought to be able to hand even Calamity Jane her needings.

"Let's go down and toss her out, Viola," suggested the chubby brunette at her right.

"Yeah," agreed the slim blonde at her left. "Hell, it's only after seven and we were late getting to bed."

The three girls started down the stairs and Calamity saw that she would have to defend herself. She put down the glass which she had taken to sip at, clenched her fists and moved to face the stair head. Taking on these three girls would whet her appetite and prepare her for dealing with Madam Bulldog when the time came.

"Hold it, Viola!"

Madam Bulldog's voice cracked out from the top of the stairs, just as her boss girl tensed ready to throw herself bodily at Calamity. The voice held the torment of the damned in it and told that, like Calamity, its owner suffered from the effects of a previous night's drinking.

Looking up the stairs Calamity focused her eyes on the owner of the Bull's Head saloon. Madam Bulldog did not look her usual cool, friendly and immaculate self on this early morning. Like Calamity, she had gone to bed fully dressed except for her head-dress and shoes; Sam, being a man of moral standing, had done no more than get his boss to her room and left her on the bed. Now she stood at the head of the stairs, bleary eyed, make-up smeared, hair hanging straggly and uncombed, not looking at all her usual self. Nor did she feel her usual self and one thing she did not want was to have her sleep shattered at this hour. The swamper had woke her by pounding on her door, he delivered an incoherent burble about some tough dame breaking into the saloon and drinking all the stock, so Madam came to investigate and found her girls already on the way down to deal with the invader.

"Come on down here, you fat old cow!" Calamity bellowed. "Can't a gal get a drink of your rotgut whisky without having to knock herself out trying to get some service?"

"You get out of here," replied Madam Bulldog, no less heatedly. "And when we open, come with a civil tongue in your head, or don't come at all."

Up until that moment Calamity had been firmly determined to leave her fight with Madam Bulldog until after she helped side Mark Counter against the Cousin's bunch. Only having a hangover always tended to make her temper as touchy as a teased rattlesnake, or even touchier.

Which was unfortunate, for having a hangover had roughly the same effect on Madam Bulldog and at the moment she, too, suffered from a hangover.

Any way one looked at it things were rapidly building up to a brawl.

"Keep out of it, you three!" growled Madam Bulldog as she started down the stairs and passed her girls. "I've got my guts full of her and her yapping. It's time we found out who's the better woman."

Silence fell on the room as Madam Bulldog carried on down the stairs to where Calamity waited with clenched fists and a mocking grin. Calamity stood ready, her eyes on the other woman's face and a feeling of eager anticipation in her heart, for this was the thing she came to Tennyson to do.

Suddenly, as Madam Bulldog came towards her, without giving any hint of what she meant to do, Calamity lashed her right fist around. The knuckles cracked against Madam Bulldog's cheek, snapping her head around and sending her staggering back into the banister at the bottom of the stair. Calamity let her breath out in a hiss, for that had been a beautiful blow.

Eagerly Calamity moved forward, ready and willing to finish off the other woman as quickly as possible. Too late she saw Madam push her plump frame from the support of the banister and shoot out a punch. Calamity walked full into it, catching the hard fist full in the face and the next instant she went reeling back, feeling and tasting the hot salty touch of blood from her lips even as she went down between two tables. She shook her head and gasped a little, for she had never before run across a woman with such a powerful punch. It looked like once more Madam Bulldog would prove to be a tougher nut to crack than she airily imagined as she rode south to try conclusions with the other woman.

Calamity came up with a bound and rushed in, fists flying. It was a tactic which carried her victorious through more than one rough-and-tumble brawl with a tough dancehall girl or cavalry camp-follower. Only this time she was up against a woman who knew more than a little about the fighting game herself. At the last moment Madam Bulldog side-stepped, rammed her left fist into Calamity's middle, then clipped her across the ear with the right as she doubled over. Calamity went down again, landing at the foot of the stairs.

"Stomp her, Madam!" howled Viola. "Hand her her needings."

Rubbing the blood which trickled from the side of her mouth, Calamity forced herself up, shaking her head. Madam was at her, one hand shooting out to dig into the girl's short hair and hold it, the other lashing in back and open palm slaps at her face. Calamity's head rocked from side to side and her own hands drove out to tangle into Madam's longer hair. The pain must have been intense if the howl Madam let out could be anything to go by. They staggered backwards across the room, both alternating between tearing at hair, swinging punches and slaps and kicking out, although as neither wore shoes this did not prove to be very effective.

It took Calamity just ten seconds to know she had tangled with a woman as strong as, and with as much fight-savvy as herself. Calamity had learned her fighting from soldiers, bullwhackers and mule-skinners and they had taught her to use her fists like a man. Wherever Madam Bulldog learned to fight, she also learned that a clenched fist proved more effective in a brawl than any amount of hair-yanking.

On the stairs the three excited saloon girls watched, gave their vocal and moral support to their boss, for Madam Bulldog had endeared herself to them all and they held her in the greatest respect. Besides Calamity Jane was not one of them, she belonged to the world outside, the world of "good women" who looked down on and sneered at the painted workers of the saloons, or caused them much trouble and inconvenience. So they wanted to see their boss hand Calamity a whipping, to uphold the high traditions of their place.

The noise brought the other girls out, sleepy-eyed and complaining until they saw what caused the fuss. Then they also settled down to enjoy the brawl. None of the male saloon workers lived on the premises, an innovation since Madam Bulldog took over, and the old swamper was hustled indignantly into a room and locked in by one of the girls. So no man saw the great battle between Calamity Jane and Madam Bulldog.

Despite the lack of witnesses, which did not bother either fighter in the least, the two women put on a brawl which neither would ever forget, nor would the few girls who saw it.

At first they fought with their fists, like two men, then closed and started hair yanking, tearing and kicking at each other, crashing to the floor and rolling over and over, still tearing at each other. They rolled apart and came up again with Calamity attacking even before Madam made her feet. She came into a punch which knocked her backwards, on to a table top. Madam rose, caught up a chair and swung it over her head, charging forward to bring it down at Calamity who rolled from the table and dropped to the floor just as the chair splintered above her and where her body had been an instant before.

With a spluttering curse Calamity dived under the table, locking her arms around Madam's legs and bringing her crashing down. Calamity clung to the legs as she fought her way to her feet, then leaned forward to grab at Madam, Too late Calamity realized she had made an error in tactics, for Madam managed to get her feet under Calamity's body. She started to thrust and Calamity, clawing desperately for a hold, caught the top of the green satin dress. With a powerful heave of her legs Madam threw Calamity backwards and from her. There sounded a harsh ripping noise as Madam's dress, tight on her figure and not meant for such strenuous activities, parted at the seams. Calamity lost her hold and shot backwards, on to a chair which broke under her and deposited her on the floor.

When Madam rose she found her torn frock impeded her free movements. She tore it from her and charged at the girl clad only in her underwear and stockings.

While still on her hands and knees, Calamity saw Madam coming into the attack. Calamity threw herself forward, her head ramming into Madam's middle and bringing a croaking gasp. Calamity locked her arms around the plump waist and bore Madam backwards.

Then a hand dug into Calamity's hair, bringing forth a howl of pain. Madam's other hand caught at the back of Calamity's shirt, tearing at it, dragging it from under the waistband of her old pants and ripping it. At that moment Madam realized such methods would do her no good and drove two hard blows into Calamity's back. The girl lost her hold and caught Madam's knee as it drove up to stagger her away. Now it was Calamity's turn to get rid of a torn garment, for the shirt got in her way. She wriggled and tore out of it without a thought for not having a stitch of clothing under the shirt. When Calamity attacked she was naked to the waist.

For a full fifteen minutes they fought like enraged wildcats and without a pause. Their clothes had suffered still more. Madam also fought bare to the waist now. In a wild thrashing attempt to grab Calamity, Madam had caught the patch on the seat of her pants, torn it away and got a hand into the exposed hole, then tore from the seat to the bottom of the right leg. Nor were clothes the only things to suffer. Neither woman had long nails, but their hard fists left bruises or drew blood, while their teeth had found flesh and both bore marks to show how effective the teeth had been. Yet, bloody, bruised, half naked and battered though both were, neither would give way or call the fight off.

Once they went down, laying gasping for breath, then slowly rose, but when they made their feet they fought on with the same ferocity which marked the fight from start to finish. They used fists, back-hand and open hand slaps rained on faces and bodies, their elbows thudded into ribs, they kicked, using the sole of the foot, they drove knees into each other, tore hair, butted like a pair of Rocky Mountain rams, threw or swung chairs at each other. Blood ran from their noses and lips, sweat soaked them, but neither gave a sign of finishing.

"Reckon we ought to stop them before they kill each other?" asked one of the watching girls as Madam and

Calamity rolled off the faro lay-out on which they had landed and thrashed over and over in their fight.

"You can try if you like," answered Viola, watching the two women, clinging to each other still, crawl to their feet and fight on. "I sure don't aim to."

"They'll stop themselves soon," another girl, face flushed with excitement, answered. Then she shuddered as Calamity swung a roundhouse punch at her boss. "Ouch! I felt that one."

Viola also winced in sympathy as Madam took the punch. It sent the plump woman stumbling back. She hit the side of the vingt-un table and clung to it for a moment, then slid down. A moan of disappointment rose from the girls as Calamity, tottering but still on her feet, started towards their boss.

"H – had – enough?" Calamity croaked, hoping the other woman would say she had.

Weakly Madam put her hand on the seat of a chair and used it to lever herself up. Her other hand gripped the edge of the table and with this to help she made her feet. She had to cling to the table, but she stood there and gasped in breath as she watched Calamity come closer.

Madam released the table and brought around her fist. The blow caught Calamity and stopped her in her tracks, for she had never thought the other woman capable of such a blow. She stood there, dazed and unable to stop the next swinging blow Madam launched against her. For a moment Madam stood staring, then swung again, this time with all her strength. Calamity's head snapped back, she reeled away, hit a table and fell over on to it, laying there.

Still Calamity was not beaten. She saw Madam coming at her and lashed out with her foot. With a flat "splat!" the foot caught Madam in the face and stopped her advance. She shook her head, another kick caught her and she stumbled forward, gripped the edge of the table and heaved it upwards. Calamity yelled as she felt herself slipping. She twisted and rolled sideways from the table as it turned over, landing on the floor and rolling over on to her back, laying there with arms thrown wide and one knee raised, her eyes glassy, her breasts heaving. On the other side of the overturned table Madam Bulldog sank to her knees, rested a hand on the floor and then flopped on to her side.

"Wowee!" gasped a girl. "They're both done for."

It certainly looked that way, for neither woman offered to try and get up for almost a minute and Viola opened her mouth to tell the others to get their boss up to her room. Before she could they all saw a movement. Only it came from the far side of the overturned table. Calamity had rolled over and braced her hands on the floor as she tried to force herself up.

"It's Calamity!" groaned one of the watching girls.

"Looks that way," agreed Viola, bitterly disappointed, for she knew that if Calamity rose she would be the winner.

Now Calamity knelt on the floor, gasping and sobbing for breath as she weakly reached her hands upwards towards the edge of the overturned table. On the other side of the table, weakly but definitely, Madam forced herself up on to her hands and knees. She could hardly think straight and wondered why Calamity had not ended the fight. She could see no sign of the girl, only the legs and bottom of the table she tipped over. The warning yells of her girls seemed to be far off and she could not make out their meaning, something about somebody getting up, pulling herself up on the table. Madam shook her head to try and clear it, then she saw a hand grip the edge of the table and another hand. Something clicked, the meaning of the yells she had heard. Although she felt like collapsing, ached in every muscle, bone and inch of flesh, although the top of her head seemed to be on fire where hands had torn at her hair, Madam Bulldog braced herself on her knees and one hand, watching the top of the table. Calamity Jane was getting up that she knew.

Calamity gripped the edge of the overturned table and used it to help drag herself to her feet. It proved to be a mistake. The moment Calamity's head came into view over the edge of the table Madam Bulldog shot out a bunched fist which crashed into the girl's jaw and sprawled her once more to the floor. Calamity rolled over and slowly tried to force herself on to her hands and knees. Just as slowly Madam rose to her feet and, staggering in exhaustion, she moved in. Bending down she took a handful of Calamity's tangled red hair and hauled her to her feet. On being released, Calamity tottered dazedly and almost fell. Before the girl's legs could collapse under her, Madam brought around a right fist with a full swing of her body, smashing it into the side of Calamity's jaw. Calamity spun around like a child's top, then crashed down. From the rag doll limp way she fell one thing was for sure – this time Calamity would not be getting up.

Stepping forward Madam sank to her knees, straddling Calamity's body, then she gripped the girl's hair in both hands, lifting the head ready to bang it against the floor. Seeing how limp Calamity's head hung in her hands, Madam released it and it flopped to the floor. Madam rested her hands on the floor by the side of Calamity's head and stayed where she was. She heard the excited chatter of the girls as they crowded down stairs and came towards her. Hands gripped her arms and helped her to her feet, for she had not the strength to rise under her own power.

"You licked her, Madam!" Viola whooped eagerly. "Come on, gals, get the boss up to her room."

Though whirling mists of pain filled her and the room seemed to be flying in a circle around her, Madam clung to consciousness. She gasped in breath to her aching, tortured lungs as her girls held her on her feet. Weakly she managed to point down to Calamity's still form as the girl lay with breasts heaving and mouth hanging open.

"G—get—her—to—her room at—h—hotel!" Madam gasped and went limp in their hands.

Mark Counter sat in the room at Doc Connel's, eating breakfast and talking over the events of the previous evening with the doctor and his uncle. Mrs. Connel, a small, pleasant woman who had many of her husband's good points, such as an ability to get things done, entered, bringing Viola with her.

"Doc," the girl gasped; she wore her street clothes and showed signs of having dressed hurriedly. "It's the boss."

"What happened?" Connel replied, thrusting back his chair and rising from the small table where he and Mark sat.

"She tangled with Calamity Jane. They fought for nearly an hour and Madam licked her in the end."

Which showed how legends could grow. The fight lasted just over thirty minutes and had already been almost doubled in duration.

"Where's Calam now?" Mark asked, also rising, for he knew something of the ways of dancehall girls with their enemies.

"We took her back to the hotel," Viola replied. "The boss told us to."

Mrs. Connel glanced at her husband. She knew and liked the boss of the Bull's Head but did not have any illusions about her toughness. If she and Calamity Jane had fought both would likely be needing medical aid. She looked at her husband and gave her orders.

"You go to the saloon and do what you can for Madam Bulldog, George. I'll take the hotel and do what I can for that Calamity Jane woman."

"I'll come along with you, ma'am," Mark offered.

"Like to see how bad ole Calam's hurt, then I'll make my rounds of the town."

"You start thinking about Cousins and his bunch arriving, Mark," warned Tune grimly. "They might be here today, or they might not. But it won't hurt none to be ready for them."

"You lie easy and I'll tend to it," Mark replied. "Say, you'll be alone for a spell. I'll put your gun under the pillow where it'll be handy."

At the hotel Mark started to follow Mrs. Connel into Calamity's room, but was ordered out before he got beyond the door.

"Tell the manager to send up some hot water," she said. "And stay out. This gal's in no state yet to have male visitors."

Mark guessed as much from the brief glimpse he'd got of Calamity before being chased out. He knew she had been wearing her sole remaining items of clothing the previous night. Which meant she would hardly be in any shape to appear in public until she obtained some more clothes.

"You'd best give me an idea of what size clothes she'd want, Mrs. Connel," he said. "Shirt and jeans."

"She a friend of yours?"

"You might say that."

"Huh!" sniffed Mrs. Connel. "There's no accounting for taste."

Mark grinned. "You're not seeing Calam at her best right now. And she's a damned good friend to have in a tight corner."

The rebuke was plain in Mark's voice and Mrs. Connel smiled. "You're right. I'm not seeing her at her best. Go tell the manager and when you get back I'll tell you the size of clothes to buy."

After delivering Mrs. Connel's message and collecting the sizes from the woman, Mark headed for the general store where the owner studied the list Mark gave him.

The items attracted some excited comment from the storekeeper who could tell at a glance the shirt and levis would never fit Mark, nor would the big Texan be likely to wear the other items of clothing on the list.

"You mean Madam 'n' Calamity Jane tangled this morning?" asked the storekeeper, sounding disappointed at missing the fight.

"That's just what I mean."

"Hell, and we never got to see it. Who won?"

"Madam, way I heard it," drawled Mark.

"Yeah, that figures," said the storekeeper, then remembered the other item of interest and speculation in Tennyson. "Say, Mark, do you reckon Cousins'll come today?"

"Today, tomorrow, the next day. He'll be here. I'll see you, Herbie."

Leaving the storekeeper loading his old ten gauge scatter gun with a dose of nine buckshot, Mark headed back to the hotel with his purchases. He went up to the first floor and tapped on the door to Calamity's room.

"How's Calam?" he asked Mrs. Connel.

"Well, one eye's closed, the other looks a mite black. Reckon she won't feel like eating anything solid for a spell way her jaw's swollen. She's got a few bites, a few lumps raised and it's easier to see bruises than skin on her body, but she'll live. That gal's sure tough as leather. She's conscious, but I've given her a dose of laudanum to ease the aches. Go in and look her over."

Mark entered the room and found a battered but clean Calamity lying on her back in the bed. By now the laudanum was taking its effect, but the girl managed a very faint attempt at her usual grin and even tried to wink through her good eye.

"You look like you tangled with a bobcat, Calam gal," drawled Mark, laying the new clothes on the chair by her bed. "And a mule or two."

For all her aching body, dulled by the laudanum's action, Calamity still tried to tell Mark what she thought of him. However the effort was too much and after an incoherent mumble she lay back and glared at him as best she could.

"Leave her be, Mark," said Mrs. Connel. "She needs rest."

"Why sure," agreed Mark and looked down at the girl. "Don't go away, Calam."

With that he left the room and found Doc Connel in the hall, having come from attending to Madam Bulldog's injuries. Mark stopped to learn how the saloonkeeper had faired in the fight.

"That must have been a hell of a brawl," Doc said. "Madam sure looks a mite peaked. I hope Cousins holds off until she gets on her feet."

"When'll that be?" asked Mark.

"I gave her laudanum to ease her aches, enough to make her sleep until noon, but she'll be stiff as a dead polecat when she recovers and in no shape for fast moving."

"Damn that fool Calam!" Mark snapped. "Why in hell couldn't she have waited a day or so. I'll take a switch to her hide, see if I don't."

After delivering the threat Mark turned and left the hotel. He walked along the sidewalk, making for the marshal's office, nodding in answer to the greetings called by passersby and owners of business premises as they opened for the day's trade. From the look of things none of them seemed unduly bothered by the threat of Cousins' arrival. Just as he was about to enter the office he happened to look towards the Wells Fargo office. He saw Viola, Madam Bulldog's boss girl, enter the building and wondered if the girl might be booking a seat, or seats, on the stage which passed through that evening headed for the west, from Sand City. He doubted if it would be Madam Bulldog running, although the injured woman might be trying to escape before Cousins arrived. Mark decided to go and see her, warn her that she could be running into more danger by leaving, for Cousins possibly would have men watching the stage coaches out of town.

Deciding he would go along to the saloon as soon as he had checked at the jail, Mark turned into the marshal's office of the jail building. His eyes went to the rack of weapons, three Winchester rifles and three double barrelled, ten gauge shotguns supplied by the town for use by the marshal and his deputies, if he ever found call to need deputies. Mark crossed to the rack and took the rifles out one after another. Much to his surprise he found they were clean and only needed loading to be ready for use. He realized that he knew little about the running of his office and would need to find out.

A check of the desk log showed his uncle had a temporary deputy, the old retired marshal, who acted as a jailer and up until the day of Mark's arrival had kept the jail and its weapons cleaned. Mark decided to pay the man a visit as he had not met him yet.

Before Mark could do this he received a visitor. The agent for the Well's Fargo office entered carrying two telegraph message forms and looking worried.

"This here's from Cousins!" he said, slapping one down before Mark. "It just now come in."

Mark took the form and read, "To the people of Tennyson. I will be coming soon. I want only Tune Counter and Madam Bulldog. Let me have them. Keep clear of me and you won't get hurt, Hank Cousins."

"Where'd it come from?" asked Mark, putting it on the desk.

"Gopher Hole way station."

"Where's that?"

"About half way between here and the place he sent the last from," replied the agent worriedly. "And that means—"

"That he could be here by noon if he pushed his horse," Mark interrupted.

"What do you want me to do with this?"

"Take it and show Mr. Hoscroft, ask him to bring the Town Council to see me."

All the time they spoke Mark watched the man's face. Something warned the big Texan that his visitor was hiding something from him. The agent turned, walked slowly towards the door, halted and came back again. His face worked with a variety of emotions as he looked at Mark. Then, as if making a difficult decision, he laid the second form on the table.

"Viola, that's Madam Bulldog's boss girl, sent this off, just afore Cousins' message came in."

"Kusin, Sand City," Mark read. "Come as soon as possible. Madam Bulldog."

He put the form down on the desk top and looked at the man. "So she's sending a message to somebody to come. What makes it so important?"

"I was on a way station with a feller called Svenson for a year," replied the agent. "We were miles from anyplace and he taught me Swedish to pass the time. I never forgot it, a man working for Wells Fargo needs to know a little of language with all the folks coming west."

"Well?"

"It never struck me, not until I got the message from Gopher Hole."

"What never struck you?" growled Mark.

"*Kusin* is Swedish for cousin."

The man looked almost sick with worry as he said this. Mark did not speak for a long moment as he thought over the import of the words. He looked down at the message form and frowned.

"Has Madam Bulldog or Viola ever sent a message to this Kusin before?" he asked.

"Nope. Only messages Madam ever sends is to likker salesmen and gals like Viola don't send telegraph messages all that often," answered the man. "What do you reckon it means?"

"I don't know."

"Why would she be sending word to Hank Cousins?" asked the man.

Mark thrust back his chair and came to his feet. The cold expression on his face caused the man to take a rapid step backwards.

"We don't know this is to Hank Cousins," Mark warned grimly. "So don't go talking about it around town."

"I didn't even aim to tell you," replied the agent indignantly.

Not for the first time since his arrival in Tennyson did Mark marvel at the devotion, friendship and respect with which many of the citizens regarded Madam Bulldog. The agent did not believe that Madam would be sending for Cousins and had clearly been undecided what he should do for the best. He had told Mark about the mysterious message as a last resort and wanted reassuring that the owner of the Bull's Head Saloon was not betraying her friends. Only Mark could not give that reassurance. From the little he had seen of Madam Bulldog he doubted if she would do such a thing as send for Cousins.

"Why would she send word to Cousins?" groaned the agent when Mark did not reply. "If it was anybody else I'd say they wanted to do a deal to save their own hide. But not Madam Bulldog."

"That's the way I see it," Mark answered. "There's nothing about the Cousins bunch to make Madam reckon they'd do a deal with her, or that they'd stick to their side of it if she made one with them."

He could see the look of relief which came to the man's face. The agent did not waste any more time, but, after stuffing away the telegraph form concerning Madam's mysterious friend in Sand City, headed out into the street to collect the town council for a meeting with Mark.

The town council came quickly. Hoscroft as mayor, the old storekeeper Mark bought Calamity's clothes from earlier, the town preacher, two more men who ran businesses in town and, although not a member of the council, the old-timer who acted as jailer.

Quickly Hoscroft introduced the council to Mark, for he had met none of them the previous day. The jailer went under the name of Corky and was a leathery old hard-case with a pair of twinkling and surprisingly young looking eyes. He hitched up the worn old Dragoon Colt slung at his side and stoutly affirmed that he stood by Mark no matter what the rest decided on doing.

"How about this message, Mark?" Hoscroft asked.

"It tells us only what we know already," Mark answered.

"All it gives us more is that Cousins is nearer than he was yesterday."

"And the message itself?" put in the storekeeper. "There's some might say we ought to do what Cousins wants, stand pat and let him make the play his way."

"Which's just what he wants," drawled Mark. "You give in to him this time and he'll walk over you, or the next bunch who wants an easy town to ride will."

"Cousins has played this hand before when he's been after somebody," Hoscroft interrupted. "Sent word ahead that he was coming and I know of one case where the town turned a man out to Cousins. This time let's show him he's bucking a town that's got guts enough to face him down."

"That's the way I likes to hear you talk, Ted," Corky growled.

"I say barricade the streets and keep men on watch ready for him!" stated the storekeeper.

"And how long could we keep them out there watching?" asked Mark. "Cousins won't be here today most likely. He want to get folks spooked, give them time to think. Nope, we can't barricade the streets or have men on guard. There's a hundred ways Cousins and his bunch could get in here after dark and we can't cover them all so as to stop them, that'd take near on a regiment of sentries and look-outs."

"What do you suggest, Ted?" the preacher asked.

Although it had become the usual thing for the town council to look to Hoscroft for suggestions, this time he did not have an answer available. He frowned and paced the room for a long minute. Mark watched, waiting to hear what the other men wished to do before he put his plans into words.

At last Hoscroft came to a halt and faced the big young Texan across the desk. Drawing in a deep breath Hoscroft put forth his thoughts and his ideas came very close to what Mark intended to ask them to do.

"What I suggest is that we appoint four special deputies to be on watch at all times in the jail under Mark and ready to go should Cousins arrive. That will give Mark a well armed fighting force at his disposal ready to stand off an attack until the rest of the town can organize."

The other members of the town council exchanged glances then looked at Mark for his views.

"That's about what I was going to ask for," Mark drawled.

"I don't have no work on," Corky grunted. "You can take me on full time if you like, Mark."

"You can be first deputy then, Corky," Mark answered. "I'll see Doc Connel and Madam Bulldog, find out if they want guards at their place."

"If I know Madam I can tell you the answer," chuckled Hoscroft. "And you'll get the same from Doc. They'll not want to take your men."

"Don't reckon we could keep it up indefinitely either," Mark said quietly. "We'll just have the four men here all the time and on the first sight of the Cousins bunch we'll get two men to the Bull's Head and two more to the doctor's. The rest of the town had best to keep off the streets, we don't want the deputies to have to wait to find out if it's a friend or not coming towards or behind him.''

"I'll see to that for you," promised the gaunt owner of the Tennyson newspaper. "For the first time since I started I'll run an extra edition."

No more time was wasted in talk. The council headed out of the office to carry out their part of the business of organizing Tennyson's defence. They agreed to get volunteers to take four hour tours of duty as deputies and that, with the exception of the preacher, they should take their turn.

For the first time Mark gave his office building a thorough examination to see how it would stand as a defensive point. After the big establishment at Quiet Town with its line of cells, large front office and a room which quartered the six man police force, Tennyson's jail looked small and puny. It had been built of stone and amounted to no more than one large room partitioned by a wooden wall. At the front side of the wall, with two windows and the double doors facing the street, lay the marshal's office. Mark passed through the partition door and found himself in a narrow passage, facing the steel barred doors of the two small cells, separated by a stout wooden wall, each with two double bunks which had been secured to the floor and each of which had a small window with two stout iron bars instead of glass.

The jail had been built for a town which could not keep a large police force and so the only door giving access to the building lay on the front street, facing the marshal's desk. Mark noted this with approval, it would save the need to have a man fully occupied with watching a rear entrance.

"It'll do," he said as he came from the cell section and found Corky seated at the desk loading the shotgun with powder and buckshot. "Seeing's how I can't get a seat at my own office I'll make the rounds. Don't you go shooting yourself in the leg.''

Corky's reply, which followed him to the door, came hot, pungent and blistering and covered the entire Counter family in its spread. Mark turned and grinned at the old-timer.

"You've been listening to Madam Bulldog," he said and left before Corky could think of an adequate reply.

Mark first went to the livery barn. He attended to his own and Calamity's horse, forgetting the girl no longer owned the big buckskin. After taking them out to the two empty corrals behind the barn and telling the owner of the establishment he would be back at nightfall and stable them, Mark went on to Doc Connel's house to see his uncle. Tune knew the town much better than did Mark and agreed with the arrangements made for its defence. Doc Connel bristlingly asserted that he did not want his office cluttered with men and that he and Tune ought to be able to take care of themselves.

"I've got a shotgun here," Doc stated grimly. "And to hell with the Hippocratic oath in Cousins' case. I didn't waste time patching this worthless cuss here up to have some murdering skunk shoot him and give me more work."

"All right, Doc," Mark grinned, seeing his uncle to be in good hands and knowing that Tune could handle his Colt if need be. "But if you hear any shooting get the house door locked. I'll be along as fast as I can."

"Sure, I'll do that," promised the doctor grimly. "I tried to get Milly to go and stay with the Hoscrofts but she won't. Danged woman, gets more ornery 'n' balky every day."

"They reckon a woman starts to take after her man," drawled Mark and left the room.

He had reached the door of the consulting room when he heard Doc's enraged yell and knew the meaning of his words had sunk in. In the sickroom Doc looked at Tune with a wry grin.

"There ain't one of you Counters to improve on the others."

"Sure ain't," answered Tune cheerfully. "That Mark's growed into a real smart man."

From the doctor's home Mark went along to the Bull's Head. He found the place open and a few customers already in. Sam left the bar and came to join Mark on catching the big Texan's signal.

"Now there's no need for you to worry, Mark," he said when Mark told of the idea for defending Madam Bulldog. "I got a ten gauge under the bar and all the waiters are heeled. The only way Cousins and his lousy buncy can get at the boss lady is through us."

"All right," Mark replied. "As soon as I hear a shot I'll bring the deputies along on the run." He grinned at Sam's surprise. "Sure, we've got deputies, a regular city police force."

"Say, I've just got a meal on order, why not set and join me?" Sam said.

Mark looked at the wall clock and found, to his surprise, the time had reached noon. He accepted Sam's offer and joined such of the saloon workers as were present at a table for a meal brought over from the café along the street. Viola was not on hand and none of the others seemed to know anything about the mysterious telegraph message the blonde sent to Sand City. Mark asked no questions about the message, for he did not want all kinds of rumors to start circulating until he got to the bottom of the matter.

A boy entered the saloon bearing a thick sheaf of newspapers fresh from the *Tennyson Herald*'s press. The arrival of an edition at this unprecedented time of the week attracted much interest and the boy sold all his copies. Mark bought one and found the editor had given the council meeting full treatment and that their advice to the citizens for when Cousins came had been printed. Mark only hoped that when the time came folks would remember and stay off the streets. If he and his deputies could pin the Cousins bunch down someplace, they could use the town's help, but not until such time.

From the talk which welled up around the saloon and the offers of help Mark received, Tennyson's citizens intended to extend a strenuous hospitality to the killer and his family. However, Mark emphasized his desire that only he and the four deputies met the first attack and folks agreed to it.

On his return to the jail Mark found his first group of special deputies gathered and waiting for him. Much to his surprise he found Stern, the blacksmith, one of the party but the burly man appeared to hold no grudge over the incident of the previous day. In fact Stern shook hands and apologized for his actions, then stated his willingness to obey orders. From what Mark saw of the man during the period they spent together the more he decided Doc Connel had been right. Stern was the kind of man who would be easily persuaded that some action be for the best and then would let himself be talked into leading the movement.

Five o'clock came around with no sign of the Cousins bunch and Mark left the jail to walk along to the Wells Fargo office and see the stage arrive. It came in a few minutes late and Mark, leaning on the wall at the end of the building, watched the door open. A big, heavily built woman climbed out. From the look of her she was a townswoman, respectable and not too well-to-do, though not poverty-stricken either. She took the big carpetbag handed to her by one of the passengers who stayed in the coach, nodded to the driver and walked along the street. Mark gave her little more than a glance, being less interested in the big blonde woman than in any other person who might climb from the coach. In this he had no luck for only the woman got down.

Mark strolled along to where the driver and agent stood talking.

"No more getting off here, friend?" he asked.

"Nope."

"Drop anybody off within a couple of miles from town?" Mark went on.

"Nope, Olaf Cussing's missus was the only one who booked anywhere near here, marshal."

"That was the blonde woman who got off?"

"Sure, her and her husband run the bath-house in Sand City. You thought I might be bringing in some of the Cousins' bunch?"

"It was a thought," agreed Mark. "See any sign on the way to town?"

"Nope, kept looking, so'd the guard," answered the driver. "Sheriff at Sand City said for me to tell you he's holding all his deputies ready to come and sit in, but he'd rather you handled it alone if you could. He's got a big gold shipment at the company office and wants to keep all his men on hand if he can."

"We'll manage then," Mark promised and was about to walk away when a thought struck him. "Say, if any of your passengers want to get off within four miles of town, make damned sure what they're fixing to do and if they can't give a real good reason for getting off hawg-tie them and come back on the run."

"I'll see to it," the driver promised.

Feeling puzzled Mark turned and headed back to the jail. It looked like the telegraph Viola sent to Sand City did not have any result. He found a fresh batch of deputies on hand, told them their duties and went to the café and had a meal. After that he headed for the livery barn to stable his and Calamity's horse for the night. With this done he headed towards the hotel to collect his bedroll, for he would be spending the night at the jail and did not see why he should spend it in discomfort.

Mark was opening his door when he heard noises from Calamity's room. He wondered if the girl's pain made her give the squeals and gasps which sounded. Mark walked to the door and listened. Calamity's crackling, profanity, interspersed by slapping sounds, squeals and little helps of pain came to his ears.

Not knowing what to expect Mark prepared to investigate. He wasted no time in knocking, that could be dangerous both to the girl and himself if something should be wrong beyond the door. His right hand brought out its Colt, then he lowered a shoulder and rammed into the door, bursting it open. Mark flung himself through the door with his revolver held ready for use.

Then Mark stood still, amazed at the scene before him. Viola staggered back a pace or two with a look of horror on her face. The woman at Calamity's bedside straightened up with a gasp of horror, her right hand still holding Calamity's ankle. On the bed, naked as the day she was born, lay Calamity. The big blonde woman who had come in on the stage let the girl's bent leg fall and took a hurried pace backwards. She no longer wore the suit she travelled to town in, now she had on an old blouse and skirt, the blouse's sleeves rolled up to show brawny arms which went well with her rather big, strong looking hands.

"Yumping yiminy!" she gasped. "What's this?"

"You all right, Calam?" Mark asked, still holding his revolver.

His words seemed to shake them out of their trance. Viola took a step forward and the big woman's face turned slightly red, her hand dropping to the neck of a bottle full of oily looking liquid which stood on the chair by the bed.

"I reckon so, Mark," Calamity replied to the question, grinning and not showing the slightest embarrassment at her lack of clothing. "If Madam Bulldog can take it I reckon I can."

"It's all right, Mark," Viola went on. "Let's you and me go out into the passage and I'll explain everything."

For a moment Mark hesitated and Calamity grinned again.

"Go on, Mark. I'm all right and you'll be making me blush next."

Holstering his Colt, Mark walked from the room and Viola followed, closing the door. From behind them came the slapping sounds, gasps and squeaks which told that the woman had started to do whatever she had been doing to Calamity all over again.

"What's this all about?" Mark asked.

"It's all right. That's Mrs. Cussing from Sand City. Madam sent for her to come here and rub her down. She's a massager."

"A what?"

"A massager. You know, one of them Swedish dames who give you a massage."

Mark grinned. "It's always been a man when it happened to me."

"Yeah, well the boss has her around once a month or so, says it keeps her schoolgirl figure. Anyway after the fight Madam decided she needed a rub down and told me to send for Mrs. Cussing. Then after she was done Madam figured that Calam'd like need some help and told me to bring Mrs. Cussing down here and tend to her."

"How do you spell Mrs. Cussings name?" asked Mark.

"K-u-s-i-n," she replied. "Why?"

"Just a thought," grinned Mark, cocking an ear towards the door through which Calamity's curses and squeals still sounded. "They always allow you have to be cruel to be kind."

He left the girl and walked to his own room. For all his grin, Mark felt relieved. Now he saw the reason for Madam Bulldog's message and the mistake in the name. In the friendly, though arbitrary way of the old west Mrs. Kusin's name became Cussing, pronounced that way by the people who saw it. That *kusin* should be Swedish for cousin amounted to nothing more sinister than coincidence, yet Mark knew how suspicion, fear, panic even, might have been spawned from the telegraph message had word of it been spread around the town. He knew his first task after he collected his bedroll must be to see the worried Wells Fargo agent and relieve the man's mind of its troubles over the message.

After satisfying the Wells Fargo agent that his trust and respect of Madam Bulldog remained unsullied, Mark went along to the jail and found his night detail of deputies present. He told them to make themselves comfortable and then made his first rounds of the night, taking Banker Hoscroft with him.

It looked more like a scene from Dodge City at the height of the trail season than the main street of a very small cowtown, to see two shotgun armed lawmen on the prowl. However the town carried on as usual, cowhands from the nearby ranches coming in and the usual assortment of drifters, visiting the Bull's Head Saloon or doing business with such stores as stayed open to catch this transient trade. The night passed without incident and the dawn came without any sign of the Cousins bunch making their arrival.

Time hung heavily on Mark's hands as he made his rounds and waited for the Cousins bunch to arrive. He hated this waiting and watching and wanted action, to get the business settled one way or the other so he could head back to the OD Connected and his friends. He did not let his nerves get on edge and kept a careful watch on the people around town to see that they did not either. He knew that nervous tension was what Cousins wanted and that the killer waited for a moment when the townsfolk were jumpy and scared, then he would strike. Only that looked as if it would be a long time in coming.

Certainly the man who rode from Tennyson shortly before noon thought the coming had been delayed long enough. So he took his horse and headed out to try and speed matters up. Although he wore a town suit he had never worked in a store or any other kind of business premises, other than a saloon or a gambling house. He came to Tennyson with Wardle and Schanz in the hope of finding the pot of gold at the end of the rainbow, or at least a town full of folk ready willing and delighted to be bilked at games of chance in which no chance was allowed on his side. The promised land did not materialize, for Tennyson had taken wise precautions against him and his kind. He stayed on even though the proposed saloon did not arrive. There were pickings for the vultures, happen a man knew how go about it and avoided coming into conflict with the law. The pickings were not great and on the day Tune Counter took lead this man had been thinking of seeking pastures new. Then he, along with Wardle and Schanz saw a chance of getting rid of Tune Counter and the strong hand which controlled the town, as well as moving Madam Bulldog from their path. By methods known to such as them, they got in touch with Cousins, notifying him of the death of his son and offering their help. In return they received word that Cousins aimed to come and take revenge and told where to look for him on his arrival. The man rode towards that place now.

For three miles he rode across country making for a large bosque well known for its qualities as a hide-out amongst men of Cousins' kind. Nor did the man from Tennyson ride blindly along. He kept a sharp watch on his backtrail, making sure no one followed him. He knew Cousins to be a most untrusting soul who would not regard the sign of approaching men with equanimity. Cousins' tricky mind might lead him to believe the leading rider had sold him out to his enemies and his answer to such an action would be effective, if crude.

At last the man, who went by the unimaginative name of Smith, halted his horse thirty yards from the edge of the woods. He scanned them for some sign of life and saw none. Being a town dweller who spent but little of his time in travelling and that time being spent in a stage coach if possible, the man called Smith thought nothing of the silence of the woods, or the lack of bird sounds.

He took out a gaudy handkerchief and mopped his face with it. Then, just as he was about to turn his horse, a thought struck him. He looked towards the silent woods and called:

"It's all right. I came alone."

Silence again, not a sound in the woods. The man licked his lips, some instinct warning him that cold eyes watched his every move. He debated to himself on the possibility of Cousins not being at the *bosque* yet and started to turn his horse to make for town.

"You'd've been dead five minutes back if you hadn't been alone."

The words came so unexpectedly that Smith almost jumped from his horse. He stared towards the *bosque* and the tall, gaunt young man in cowhand clothes who stepped from behind a tree, cradling a Winchester rifle across his arm.

"I'm a friend of Charlie Wardle," Smith said hurriedly, smiling what he hoped was a warm and winning smile. "You with Hank Cousins?"

"You might say that."

"Charlie told me where to come," Smith explained.

A cold, wolf-savage smile split the young man's face and he gestured with his rifle. "Come and come easy. I'd as soon shoot you as not."

With that friendly advice given the young man turned on his heel and walked away into the trees. Smith swung down from his horse and led it as he followed the lead of his guide.

After winding through the trees of the *bosque* for a time they came at last to where, in a hollow on the banks of a stream, a small, rough camp had been made. Five men were by the small campfire and they came to their feet, hands reaching to their guns as they looked with suspicious gaze at Smith. Three of the men showed a strong family likeness, the burly man with steel rimmed spectacles being Hank Cousins. Next to him stood the oldest son, Burt, a mean looking unshaven man. Ted and Joe, the look-out, were twins and neither would have won any prize for having a kind or gentle facial aspect. The remaining two men had all the marks of hard-case outlaws, men who would follow any leader as long as he paid well and would stay loyal to him until it came to a time when loyalty no longer paid them.

"What're you wanting?" Hank Cousins asked, coldly surveying Smith through the plain glass of his spectacles.

"I was in with Wardle and Schanz," replied Smith.

"Why didn't they come themselves?" growled Cousins, then looked at Joe and didn't wait for Smith's reply. "Was he followed?"

"Naw."

"I made sure of that," Smith stated. "Wardle and Schanz got themselves run out of town and I thought I'd come along to let you know how things stand."

"Did you?" asked Cousins with a chilling lack of interest.

"Sure. The folks there are standing fast, all of them are solid behind the marshal."

"The marshal's hurt bad," said Cousins, "or so we was told."

"His nephew come in and took over. A big *hombre* toting a brace of white handled guns that he's real fast with. He beat Al Cordby to the shot in a fair fight, which same Cordby was drawing first when he got it."

A low rumble of talk came from the men and a quick exchange of glances which told Smith he had interested the others. They all knew Cordby's reputation and were wondering who this fast-drawing nephew of Tune Counter's might be. Then one of the two non-Cousinses recollected something.

"Counter," said the man, Potts by name, "he

wouldn't be a real big, handsome blond haired feller, would he?''

"That's him," agreed Smith.

"And that's *Mark* Counter," Potts went on, then as if he thought more explanations might be needed. "Dusty Fog's *amigo*."

Now all the others were interested. Dusty Fog's name stood high amongst the real fast men in Texas.* Cousins and his bunch all knew the close ties of friendship and loyalty between Dusty Fog and the other members of the OD Connected crew, and Mark Counter belonged to that crew; more he belonged to the élite of the crew, the floating outfit, and his name had often been linked with Dusty Fog.

"Is either Dusty Fog or the Ysabel Kid with him?" asked the second man, Jacobs by name.

Not being a Cousins he did not have any particular stake in this game, he had no kin to avenge and came along merely in case there should be a chance to loot some place in town. He most certainly had not come along to tie into fuss with Dusty Fog, Mark Counter and the Ysabel Kid.

"There's only Mark Counter in Tennyson right now," Smith answered, then an inspiration struck him. "He sent for the others, they're due here tomorrow."

Cousins scowled at the others. He would have preferred to handle the matter of avenging his son with just his kin, but felt the need for a couple of extra guns to back him. He had planned to stay on out here for another couple of days to really give the folks time to stew on his threats. He had used the same system before when meaning to hit a town. The telegraph messages stirred things up, his blood-thirsty reputation did the rest. A couple more days of anxiety would see folks in Tennyson debating the futility of resistance, even with a good man to back them. Yet if Dusty Fog and the

* *Dusty Fog's history is given in the author's floating outfit novels.*

Ysabel Kid should arrive they would effectively stiffen the town in such a manner that no amount of threatening telegraph messages would worry them.

"We go in tonight," he said, reaching the decision Smith hoped to get. "Show me the layout of the town."

Reaching into his pocket Smith produced a copy of the *Tennyson Herald* and passed it to Cousins. He stood watching the killer read the town council's orders to the population. At last Cousins crumpled the paper in his hands, then tossed it to the ground.

"Smart!" he snarled. "Too damned smart for a bunch of hick yokels. This's Mark Counter's doing."

"He had the town council in to see him yesterday," Smith answered. "They've appointed four special deputies who're on watch all the time day and night at the jail house. There's one thing though. The jail's only got one way out, straight on to the main street."

The significance of the words did not escape Cousins. He scuffed his boot toe over the soil at his feet, making a clear level area to which he pointed.

"Show me how the town lays," he ordered.

Taking a stick Smith squatted on his heels and started to make as good a map as he could manage under the conditions. He tried to show the full lay-out of the town, pointing out the salient points, such as the jail, the saloon and Doc Connel's house. Despite his lack of experience as a map-maker Smith gave Cousins a very clear idea of what he would run into when he reached Tennyson.

"How bad is Tune Counter hurt?" he asked.

"Pretty bad, by all accounts. And from what I heard Madam Bulldog tangled with Calamity Jane yesterday. They're both still in bed."

"You mean they had a tooth 'n' claw brawl?" asked Tad Cousins.

"So the word has it. Only the saloon gals know for sure what happened. I was in there last night and the gals all talked about the fight, it was a real humdinger from what they say and I can well believe it.''

"You don't know for sure about it then?'' Hank Cousins put in.

"Nope,'' Smith replied. "Calamity came in with Mark Counter and tied in with Madam Bulldog, got out-cussed, lost near on all she stood up in at poker, then got herself drunk under the table a couple of nights back. We all expected her to be back r'aring to go last night, but she never showed, so I reckon it's true what the gals said about being a fight.''

Cousins' usual scowl deepened as he looked Smith up and down. He did not know the man and wondered just what Smith expected to gain out of helping him. How far he could trust Smith, or even if he could trust Smith at all, Cousins did not know. He looked the man over with cold eyes and asked:

"Just what do you reckon to gain out of all this?''

"A saloon and good pickings. With Madam Bulldog and Tune Counter gone I'll get them both, provided your boys don't bust up the saloon too much. Which same's why I come out here, to see if you thought my help'd be worth not busting up the place.''

"You want us to kill Tune Counter and Madam Bulldog for you?'' sneered Burt Cousins.

"You're going to kill him, and Madam Bulldog anyhow,'' Smith replied. "I reckoned that if I did you a favor you'd do me one in return.''

None of the men spoke for a long moment. Hank Cousins for one felt better about Smith now the matter had been put into terms he could understand. Smith stood to make money out of the deaths of two people and Cousins could see why the man would offer his help. He made his decision and prepared to tell the others his plan. He had one thing to attend to before he made any plans.

Looking at Smith, he pointed to the trees. "Get going!'' he said.

"What—!'' yelped the startled man.

Coming forward fast Joe Cousins thrust the barrel of his rifle hard into the middle of Smith's back.

"You heard pappy?" he asked. "Walk – or stay put permanent."

"Don't gun him unless you have to!" Cousins barked, being under no delusions about Joe's regard for human life.

Not until Smith, protesting his friendship, departed, did Hank Cousins offer to tell his men his ideas for taking the town of Tennyson. He did not doubt that Smith had his interests at heart, especially as Smith stood to gain by those same interests. However, the less Smith knew the less he could tell should he be caught out and questioned. Smith did not strike Hank Cousins as being the most staunch of men and would crack under forceful treatment, so the less he knew about Cousins's plans the better the outlaw liked it.

"It could be a trap," Potts said quietly.

"Reckon it is, Hank?" asked Jacobs.

"Nope, Smith wants that saloon bad and we're going to hand it to him. We're headed in tonight."

"How?" asked Burt.

"Quiet and easy. I'll tend to Tune Counter myself. Joe and Tad take the saloon and hand Madam Bulldog her needings. Should be easy enough with her off her feet. Even if she's back on them likely she'll be too stiff 'n' sore to make any fast moves."

All the others exchanged glances, for they'd heard what the wounded man who escaped the hold-up had to say on the subject of Madam Bulldog's way with a gun. Burt looked at his father.

"How about me, paw?"

"You, Potts and Jacob's be hid out opposite the jail, with your rifles. I'm counting on you to hold Mark Counter and the deputies inside if there's only the one door. To save us starting ahead of each other, Tad, don't you start shooting until nine o'clock, that's the time we'll be in town. By ten past nine we'll be riding out and both Tune Counter 'n' Madam Bulldog'll be dead.''

Calamity Jane stood in her hotel room and lifted her arms over her head, standing so she could see herself in the mirror. Her body still looked mottled by the various bruises and abrasions but she flexed her arms and had no stiffness in them. It said much for Mrs. Kusin's skill as a masseuse that Calamity could move with such ease after the fight she had fought with Madam Bulldog. Three times Mrs. Kusin had come to Calamity's room and worked on her, probing, rubbing, slapping until the girl felt like she had been through the fight all over again. Now it was all over, the stiffness and aches no longer bothered Calamity and she felt the time had arrived when she must take up the cudgel and try conclusions with Madam Bulldog once more.

She took up the clothes Mark bought for her and dressed, grinning as she found the shirt to be a size larger than she usually wore. Once fully dressed she took up her old Navy Colt, checked that it still carried its loads, rested the butt on her knee and slipped percussion caps on to the nipples, set the hammer on the safety notch between two of the loaded chambers and thrust the gun into her waistband. She made sure of the set of the weapon, put her battered cavalry kepi on at a rakish angle and left her room whistling an old army tune.

A meal was Calamity's first requirement and she got this in the hotel's dining room. Then she left, walked out into the street and headed for the Bull's Head. The first thing she noticed on leaving was the deserted aspect of the town. Along the street only the Bull's Head saloon and the marshal's office carried lights to show they were open for business. Not a horse stood at any hitching rack and nobody walked the streets.

Knowing the west, Calamity could read the signs. Tennyson expected trouble. She could smell it in the air, feel it all around her. The citizens had closed their business premises and most likely stayed at home, loaded weapons ready to their hands as they had done in the old days when the Kiowa and Comanche Indians rode the plains.

Although she had thought of visiting Mark Counter and seeing if she could do anything to help him, Calamity overlooked one vital detail. The Bull's Head lay between the hotel and the marshal's office. At the saloon's hospitable doors she paused, then turned and entered.

Her foot barely touched the floor inside when she froze, hands at her sides. The saloon contained only half a dozen townsmen for customers, but the full force of waiters, dealers and bartenders stood around and all of them wore guns. Guns towards which their hands dropped as she entered.

"Hi!" she greeted, unperturbed by the way the men watched her. "Don't shoot until I've had me a drink."

The hostile looks faded away and the men relaxed, although Viola and the few girls in the room threw scowls at the grinning Calamity as she headed for the bar. They might have shown their dislike in a more practical way, but Madam Bulldog had given definite orders which Viola passed on.

"You looking for trouble, Calam?" asked Sam, sliding a beer along the bar top towards the girl.

"*Me?*" she replied, looking innocent as a dove cooing in a peach tree. "Why I never look for trouble. Where at's the boss?"

"Be down soon."

Calamity caught the glass and raised it to her lips. "First since the last," she remarked, then looked around the room. "You're sure slack tonight."

"Yeah," Sam replied and let it go at that, for he sure wanted to keep his eyes on the door.

Time passed and at ten to nine Calamity heard a sound at the head of the stairs. She looked up to see

Madam Bulldog at the top and just starting to walk down, moving with her usual light footed, rubbery grace which told that Mrs. Kusin's handling had been just as successful as in Calamity's case. Only this night Madam did not wear her working dress. She wore a black two-piece ladies' suit with a frilly fronted white blouse. Calamity saw under the left side of the jacket as Madam Bulldog started to come downstairs. The saloonkeeper carried a revolver under her arm in a shoulder clip.

Before Madam reached the bottom, the batwing doors opened and two men stepped in, two men with drawn revolvers in their hands. They timed the move just right, for just at that moment all eyes had gone to Madam Bulldog.

"Sit tight, all of you!" snapped Tad Cousins.

"Do it, or we throw lead into the gals before you get us!" Joe Cousins went on. "We're looking for Madam Bulldog."

Their threat worked. The men might have taken a chance, but not to endanger Viola and the other girls' lives.

"I'm the one you want," said Madam Bulldog, coming slowly down the stairs and stepping forward to face the two men. "The rest of them aren't in this."

"You're her, huh?" grunted Joe and started to move his gun around.

At that moment Calamity Jane thrust herself from the bar, ignoring the gun Tad turned towards her. She pointed at Madam Bulldog and glared defiantly at the Cousins' brothers.

"Hold it!" she snapped. "Listen, you pair, I don't know what's between you and her, but I got first claim on her. This fat old cow cold-decked me out of all I own at cards, hocussed my fire-water, then, when I come back the next morning for a reckoning, her and three of her calico cats jumped me and worked me over. So I've got me a gun and come looking for her. And I'm damned if I'll stand back to let a couple of ringtailed rippers come in and take her from me."

"Reckon you can take her?" asked Joe.

"You reckon I can't?" Calamity spat back. "Just stand back and leave me try."

Joe threw a glance at the clock. By now his father would have the men staking out the jail house and be well on his way to Doc Connel's house. He flashed a glance at Tad who grinned and nodded. They did not object to committing a cold-blooded murder, but knew every man for hundreds of miles would be out after them if they killed a woman, especially a well-liked and respected woman like Madam Bulldog. If they let Calamity Jane do the killing it would serve their purpose and all blame fall on the girl. From the look of Calamity and Madam Bulldog they sure had tangled and as none of the girls showed signs of injury it looked like Calamity got licked fair and now made loser's music. If the girl tried and failed to kill Madam, then they could still cut in and finish the job.

"Get to it!" Tad ordered. "Nobody else move."

On receiving permission Calamity turned to face Madam. Her hand lifted to hover the butt of the Navy Colt. Madam moved around to stand squarely facing her, her eyes on the girl's face, the good one trying to read some sign of warning that Calamity was about to make her draw.

Behind the bar Sam threw a look at his ten gauge. He swore an oath to himself that, even if he died in doing it, he would cut Calamity in two pieces with a load of blue-whistlers should she throw down on and kill his boss.

"When you're ready, Madam," Calamity said calmly.

Unaware of the developments around them, Mark Counter and his deputies sat around the desk and in a low stake, but highly enjoyable, poker game. Mark tossed his hand into the pot with an expression of disgust and rose from the desk.

"About time you lost one," snorted old Corky. "See now how you pay your deputies so good. You take it off 'em playing poker."

Mark grinned and paced the room while waiting for the next pot. He knew he would have a fair wait, for Corky had become a long-winded card player given to much deliberation before making any move, even if the move be the simple act of folding and tossing into the deadwood in the table center. So Mark strode the length of the room and turned. In doing so he chanced to glance out of the window.

That one glance told him the long awaited moments of action had come. It also warned Mark that he had made an error in tactics. He had one man in the rear cells, watching the back of the jail, but unless he was badly mistaken they were held prisoner inside the jail building.

What he had seen was two men standing in the alley between the two opposite buildings. More, he had seen one start to raise a rifle but be restrained by the other.

Mark did not panic. He knew he must think fast, for the Cousins bunch had at last reached Tennyson and even now would be moving. He crossed the room in the same relaxed and casual manner he had done several times before and threw a glance at the alley at the other end of the facing building. Sure enough another man stood at it, rifle in hand. That meant they were not just casual idlers even if the prevented raising of the rifle had not already told Mark as much.

He crossed to the desk and rested his hands on top, looking at the men. He stood with his back to the front windows so the men outside would not be able to guess what he aimed to do.

"Don't get up, or look," he said. "There's three men with rifles outside. They've got us bottled in."

To give them credit, not one of the men at the table gave the slightest sign of surprise, or of being aware that the watchers had them pinned in with the only way out under easy range for a rifle.

"What're we going to do, Mark?" Cork asked. "This means Cousins's in town."

"I know," Mark replied. "We've got to get out."

"Won't be easy," growled Corky. "Could try rushing 'em."

"They'd cut us down as we went through the door," Mark answered.

"I allus reckoned this place should have a back door," growled one of the deputies.

Mark looked at his hands, then at the men. "So do I. Keep on playing like we didn't know they were there."

He passed back through the door into the cells section where Hoscroft sat in a cell and watched through the rear window. The banker, taking his turn like the rest at the most boring of all the jail duties, looked at Mark as the big Texan entered the cell.

"What's wrong?" he asked.

"Cousins's playing it smart. Got us bottled, three men out front. Just move to one side and leave me room to work."

Taking up his shotgun Hoscroft watched Mark approach the window and take a firm hold of the bars, one in each hand. Then Mark lifted his right leg and pressed the sole of his foot against the wall.

"You'll never do it, man!" Hoscroft gasped when he saw Mark's intention.

Mark did not reply to this. His enormous muscles started to bulge and writhe as he strained with all his might against the strength of the stonework surrounding the bars. Never had Hoscroft seen such grim determination shown on a man's face and Mark applied all his might and power against the bars. Sweat poured down Mark's face but he kept up that steady, yet power packed pull on the iron. He felt as if his lungs must crack, yet still held on and still his leg forced against the side of the cell.

"You can't do it," Hoscroft began, "No man c—!"

At that moment the words trailed off, for he became aware of a steady trickle of powder running from a thin crack at the side of the window. He realized what this powder must be. Concrete crushed up by the pressure. He stared and saw the very framework of the window begin to quiver.

"Warn the others!" Mark gasped, relaxing for an instant before a final effort.

Without needing other instructions Hoscroft left the cell. He entered the front office acting like a sentry relieved for a cup of coffee. While pouring his drink he told the others what Mark planned to do. They showed no sign of the tension all were under, but sat ready, though they doubted if even Mark could do it.

Inside the cell Mark drew in a deep breath and took a firm hold of the bars once more and put on the pressure. Slowly, so slowly that it appeared nothing would happen, the stone gave. With a rumble and clatter the bars and their framework were torn from their bed. Mark lowered the heavy frame to the ground and leaned against the wall breathing heavily.

Hoscroft came in fast, staring unbelievingly at the torn gash where the window had been. Mark rested against the wall for a moment then turned and said:

"Pass me the shotgun. I'll get around the side."

Before the other men could make any objection Mark slipped out through the window. He took the shotgun Hoscroft passed through, drawing back both hammers and checking that the percussion caps sat ready for use.

"Get ready," Mark ordered. "I'll take the two, they're on the side nearest to the saloon and Doc's house. Once I start shooting get the windows bust and cut loose. There's no time to waste."

He turned and headed around the corner of the building out of sight. Moving his feet carefully, feeling for anything against which he might kick and cause a clatter which would warn the watchers across the street, Mark kept to the shadows. Knowing there to be no door at the rear of the building, the men at the other side never suspected a thing until he almost reached the corner. Then one saw him and let out a yell, throwing his rifle up. Fast taken or not, his bullet kicked chips from the wall close to Mark's head. The big Texan did not hesitate, the ten gauge in Mark's hands boomed out a reply to the rifle. He saw the man jerk back as buckshot ripped into him, stagger and hit his pard even as the second man tried to get his rifle up, Mark changed his aim slightly and emptied the other barrel. He heard the man scream, heard also the shattering glass and the roar of a rifle from the jail front and knew Hoscroft or one of the others must have been ready and waiting to cut in.

There was no time to waste. Mark dropped the empty shotgun, for he saw both his men lay on the ground. He did not know how badly hurt they might be, but he had to get to Connel's house as quickly as possible. Madam Bulldog had men to help her and the doctor stood alone.

One of the two men Mark cut down with the buckshot rolled clear of the other. It was Burt Cousins, and the outlaw, snarling with agony-filled rage, gripped and brought up his rifle, aiming on the big Texan as he sprang from the side of the jail and ran down the street. Even as Cousins took aim old Corky burst from the jail holding his old Dragoon, the gun roared like a cannon and Cousins lifted almost to his feet under the impact of the lead, then dropped, draping himself across the still body of Potts.

At the other end of the building Jacobs decided discretion to be the better part of valor, turned and ran for safety.

Calamity Jane's eyes locked Madam Bulldog's as the girl tried to pass a message. Calamity winked with her good eye, the eye on the side away from the Cousins brothers, but Madam gave no sign of knowing, or even seeing the wink.

"Take her, Calamity!" Cousins snarled. "Or we will."

At that same moment they all heard the thunder of shots from along the street. Joe and Tad Cousins threw quick glances at the wall clock, for it wanted five minutes to nine o'clock and they knew their father could not have reached Connel's house yet. More, the shots sounded from the wrong way. It seemed that Burt had run into trouble down at the jail. For an instant both men's guns wavered out of line.

"Now!" yelled Calamity.

She pivoted around, hand lashing to the butt of her Navy Colt. If Madam had not read her sign right she would damned soon know about it.

Madam Bulldog's right hand shot across, under her left jacket side, closed on the grip of the Cloverleaf and brought it out. A split second after Calamity's move, Madam also turned. She saw the brothers trying to bring their guns into line just as her gun barked – a flicker of a second before Calamity's Navy Colt spoke.

Too late the two outlaws tried to get their guns into line. Tad sent a wild shot into the bar between the two women, then Calamity's Navy bullet struck him. An instant ahead of Calamity's shot, Joe took a .41 ball in the chest and reeled back. He kept his feet and tried to line a gun. A ragged volley tore from the weapons held by Madam's male workers, drawn the moment they saw a chance. Joe hit the wall, almost torn to doll-rags by the lead.

Still on his feet Tad stumbled back through the bat-wing doors. He heard running feet approaching, pounding along the sidewalk towards him. Turning, he saw a big blond man wearing a marshal's star who came sprinting at him. Snarling in rage Tad tried to raise and use his gun.

Mark Counter saw Tad erupt from the saloon after hearing the shots. Saw also the gun Tad held and drew left handed, firing on the run. Twice his long barrelled Army Colt bellowed. Tad reeled back under the impact, hit the batwing doors and fell inside.

"It's Mark Counter coming by!"

The yell left Mark's throat as he holstered his Colt and landed on the board walk before the Bull's Head. He did not wish to get shot by someone inside under the mistaken impression he belonged to the Cousins gang.

"We got the other one!" came back an answering yell. Calamity Jane's voice or Mark missed his guess.

He did not stop, for the most dangerous of all the Cousins bunch was headed after his uncle.

Hank Cousins heard the shots even as he ran towards Connel's house, after making a round trip keeping well clear of the backs of the houses. He heard the rifle, then the boom of the shotgun. He heard other shots just as he started to mount the stairs leading to Connel's surgery. The meaning of the shots became clear to him. His plan had slipped somehow, failed and his boys were in trouble. Then he heard Mark's yell and caught the muffled reply. If Mark Counter had escaped from the jail his son Burt must be dead. This thought received stronger confirmation by the fact that no more shots sounded by the jail and Burt would die fighting.

Snarling in rage Cousins halted in his climb. His three sons had been killed and his own chances of getting Tune Counter, and escaping after it, sank to lower than zero. He must get away, gather a big bunch around him and sweep down on Tennyson in a raid which would make Quantrill's attack on Lawrence, Kansas, look like a Sunday-school outing.

Cousins turned and started down the steps, his gun in his hand. He saw Mark burst into sight around the edge of the next house. With a snarl he brought up his gun to take a careful sight.

Against a lesser man it might have worked. Mark saw

the shape against the white wall of Connel's house. Saw it and went down in a dive, fetching clear his right hand Colt (he had holstered the other to run the easier) even as he fell. He heard Cousins' bullet slap over his head, then he lit down and his left hand started to fan the hammer of the Colt. The shots thundered out like the roar of a Gatling gun. Splinters kicked from the bannister above Cousins, inched nearer for two more shots even as he aimed again. Just before Cousins touched off the shot Mark's next bullet caught him and caused his lead to fly harmlessly into the air. Twice more Cousins rocked under the impact of the lead, then slowly, almost reluctantly it seemed, his body crumpled forward and fell to the ground, his gun clattered down the steps away from him.

Coming to his feet Mark walked forward, holstering his empty right hand Colt and drawing the weapon from his left holster. He saw the door at the head of the stairs burst open. Connel and two men appeared, all holding weapons, they looked down at the body, then towards Mark, who hurriedly called out so they would recognize him and not throw lead.

The men closed in on Cousins' body, keeping their weapons ready for use but they did not need the precaution, for the outlaw would never rise again, not after being torn almost in two pieces by three bullets from Mark's Army Colt.

"Landsakes," said Calamity Jane, looking at the circle of faces around the bar. "I was like to pee my pants when I jumped them Cousins boys. I wasn't sure you get my meaning, Madam."

"I wasn't sure I had either," Madam replied. "But I figured to take at least one of them with me."

The time was half past ten and Tennyson lay peaceful again, the bodies of the Cousins bunch on slabs at the undertaker's shop. Now a crowd of citizens gathered at the Bull's Head and Mark Counter stood with his "deputies", Madam Bulldog and Calamity Jane, talking over the events of the evening.

"You mean you aimed to get one of the Cousins boys even if Calam cut you down?" Hoscroft asked.

"Sure, way I saw it Sam there was all set to settle Calam," replied Madam Bulldog calmly.

"You can't trust nobody these days," grinned Calamity, not at least worried by her narrow escape. "Like to say one thing though. Madam licked me fair and square at everything, including shooting, way I saw it. One thing nobody's going to say is that lil ole Martha Jane Canary's a poor lo—"

Madam Bulldog's glass fell from her hand. She stared at Calamity's face for a moment after the girl announced her full name. Then Madam's hands shot out to grip Calamity by the shoulders.

"What did you say your name was?" she asked.

"Martha Jane Canary," Calamity answered, lowering her fists which she had clenched ready to defend herself.

"Oh, my god!" gasped Madam Bulldog.

Her face lost its color, her hands dropped from Calamity's shoulders and she went down in a limp heap on the floor. Mark bent and scooped the woman up while Viola dashed up and Sam came over the counter top in a bound.

"What happened?"

At least a dozen voices asked the same question. Calamity stared at Mark as he held the woman's limp body in his arms.

"She fainted!" croaked Calamity. "Get her into her office, Mark."

A pale faced Madam looked at Mark, Sam, Viola and Calamity in her office. She managed a wry smile.

"Sorry if I scared you. I'd like to see Calam alone for a few minutes, please. It'll be all right."

The few minutes lasted for half an hour and when Calamity came out of the office she looked strangely subdued. She crossed to where Mark stood and wiped a hand across her brow.

"Sure she's all right," Calamity replied to various inquiries. "The evening's been a mite too much for her. Coming down to the hotel, Mark?"

"Yeah. I may as well."

They walked along the street side by side and Calamity looked up at him as they passed the end of the Bull's Head Saloon.

"When you riding out, Mark?" she asked.

"In a couple of days. Old Corky can keep things under till Uncle Tune gets back on his feet and there's likely to be work waiting for me at the OD Connected."

"I'm going in the morning."

"Can let you have a couple of hundred to stake you until you get a start again," Mark said.

"Thanks, *amigo*," she replied. "Only Madam's give me back all she won from me, so I don't need it."

"A fine woman all round," Mark drawled.

"Real fine. We talked for a fair piece. I'm going to tell you something, Mark, only it's something I don't want to get out."

"You know me, old Clam Counter they call me."

Calamity laughed, then she hooked her hand under his arm.

"I should have figured it when she out-cussed me, licked me at poker, drunk me under the table and then whipped me," she said quietly, looking more subdued than Mark could ever remember seeing her look before.

"Guessed what?" he asked.

"There could only be one gal who's that much better than Calamity Jane. Madam Bulldog told me her name tonight. It's been so long that neither of us recognized each other."

"What the hell are you on about?" Growled Mark.

"Madam Bulldog. Her real name's Charlotte Canary."

Mark stopped in his tracks, turning the girl to face him. "C – Canary?" he gasped.

"That's right as the Injun side of a hoss," Calamity grinned. "The only gal who could whup me the way she did would have to be my mother."

PART TWO

The Gamblers

DUSTY FOG, THE Ysabel Kid and Waco had agreed unanimously that Mark Counter was the best man for the job although Mark objected most strenuously to getting it. They ruled out his objections on several counts. In the first place Mark's satorial elegance exceeded any of their own, which he could not truthfully deny. Secondly, Mark owned all the necessary items of clothing for such an occasion; so did both Dusty and the Kid, but they claimed Mark looked so much better in his. Waco said he did not own any such fancy low-necked clothes and hoped he never would, so that let him out of it. Thirdly, and perhaps most important, Dusty and the Kid had already sampled Brenton Humboldt's hospitality and thought Mark ought to take his fair turn.

"It looks to me like you've caught it then, Mark," said Ole Devil Hardin when the members of his floating outfit stopped their talking. "I'm sorry to land it on you and I never expected any of it when I put my money into Humboldt's meat-packing plant. I hoped that finished me with it, apart from drawing in my share of the profits and never thought he'd write and ask me to send my representative along to his daughter's wedding."

"Maybe he wants backing in some other idea," drawled the Kid who suffered no illusions about Brenton Humboldt's true nature.

"You be sure to apologize for Lon and me, Mark," grinned Dusty. "Tell Humboldt we're both suffering the miseries through having a touch of the grippe."

121

"It'll be bad enough going there for you without telling your lies as well," Mark answered. "I'll pull out in the morning."

"For a feller as doesn't want to go up there, *amigo*," the Kid put in dryly, "you're sure in a tolerable hurry to get started."

"Why sure," agreed Mark. "I could make it in maybe four days' hard riding. But I don't aim to try. I've been sent out on this chore against my will so I aim to travel easy and sleep under a roof every night as I go."

The others laughed. They knew all too well that Mark hated sleeping out of doors. Even the fact that he spent much of his life using the ground for a mattress and the sky for a roof did not make him like it any the more. So he planned to make a leisurely journey of it and spend each night in a town, ranch house or line cabin. To do so would need careful arranging and involve swinging and swerving instead of riding in a near enough straight line.

At dawn the following morning Mark rode away from the OD Connected house. In his war-bag, packed neatly and rolled in the protection of his blanket's suggans and tarp, Mark carried his cutaway coat, white frilly bosomed shirt, town style trousers and shoes. If he must attend the wedding he intended to be dressed at his best.

Three days later, shortly after the sun went down, Mark hung his saddle on an inverted V-shaped wooden framework, known as a burro, in the stable of the Bella Union Hotel at Culver Creek. His big bloodbay stallion stood in a loose box and Mark glanced at the two fine looking harness horses standing in the adjacent stalls. He drew the Winchester Model '66 rifle from his saddleboot and threw a glance at the light two-horse carriage which stood at the side of the big stable building.

"Fine rig," he said to the old-timer who slouched towards him, pitchfork on shoulder.

"Mighty fine picture it made coming in, too," replied the man. "With them two high-stepping bays hauling it and that right pretty looking woman driving. She sure could handle them."

"She staying at the hotel?"

"Sure," answered the man, waving a hand to the trunk lashed on the back, "I don't know how long for though. Telled me to leave the trunk for today, so's she could see how she liked the look of the town. Me, I says, 'Lady', I says, 'happen you take time out to look at this here town you won't stay at all.' "

"What'd she say?" Mark asked, knowing stable workers to be inveterate gossips who could lick barbers for passing on information or news.

"Just laughed and walked off with one fair sized bag. Sure don't know who she is or what she's doing out here, but I never heard an accent like she'd got afore."

"She a saloon gal?"

"What, with a rig and team like that?" scoffed the man. "Naw, she's maybe some rich eastern gal out west looking for a husband. There's a chance for you, happen you'd like a wife."

"I wouldn't," grinned Mark.

"Or me – trouble is I've got one."

Carrying his bedroll and rifle, Mark walked away from the chuckling man. At the hotel's reception desk Mark booked a room for the night and took the key, then headed upstairs. He came to the passage with the hotel rooms on either side and saw from the numbers that he would be at the end of the passage, so he walked towards his room's door.

The door facing Mark's room opened just as he walked towards it and one of the most beautiful women Mark had ever seen stepped out. Mark was something of a connoisseur of female pulchritude and found nothing in the young woman's appearance to offend his predilections. She had hair as golden blonde as his own, not too long or too short and neatly combed and cared for. The fact was as near perfection as a man could ask for, holding an intelligent, calm and somewhat regal expression, the blue eyes meeting Mark's with neither shyness nor boldness, looking him over coolly. She wore a cloak which effectively hid whatever kind of dress lay under it, yet conveyed the idea that it would pay a man to unwrap the cloak and look.

Mark nodded a greeting. Carrying his rifle in one hand and bedroll in the other he could not remove his hat. She replied with a calm, grave "Good evening", and carried on down the passage out of his sight. Mark watched her go before entering his room. It did not need a Comanche witch-woman's powers to guess this beautiful blonde woman must be the owner of the carriage and pair of horses he had seen. He had heard only two words and yet he could near enough swear she spoke in the accent of an upper-class Britisher such as he had run across on a few occasions.

After washing and shaving in his room, and leaving his rifle by the bed, Mark headed downstairs to the hotel dining-room, hoping to see the woman again, perhaps even get to know her and satisfy his curiosity. In this he was disappointed, for the woman did not appear to be in the room. Mark asked the waiter and learned she left earlier bound on some business of her own.

So, after a good meal, Mark left the hotel and took his first look at Culver Creek. The first thing which struck him was the size of the town. Serving as a convenient fording spot of the Culver Creek of the Brazos River, the town found a lucrative source of income in trail herds headed north as well as being the center of a thriving cattle area and having a large, well manned Army post within easy distance of it. All this gave Culver Creek a more pretentious atmosphere than might be expected in a Texas cowtown. Certainly the General

Hood Saloon looked more in keeping with one of the better areas of Dodge City than a small town.

On entering the saloon Mark found himself surprised at the trade it drew, for there appeared to be a goodly crowd enjoying themselves in the big barroom, a mixed crowd of cowhands and soldiers. Both the army post and the local ranches appeared to have paid their men on the same day and the same men vied eagerly with each other to get rid of a good portion of their month's pay in one glorious night of fun and frolic.

Passing across the room, Mark came to a halt at the bar and a glass of beer slid along to his order. He took it up and spent a couple of minutes in looking around the room in the hope he might see someone he knew. However, the gambling tables, the groups of men gathered with the saloongirls in drinking, laughing and talking parties, failed to yield a friendly, or even a casual acquaintance to his gaze and so Mark, who never liked drinking alone, decided he would finish the beer then head back to his room. He did not care for the atmosphere of the place. It seemed to carry all the money-grabbing intensity of a trail-end town joint making hay while the Texas trail hand sun shone, and bore none of the homely feeling of a small town saloon which also served as an informal social club for the cowhands.

"Howdy friend," said a voice from behind Mark.

Turning to see who addressed him, Mark found himself being favored with the attentions of somebody who must be either the owner, or floor manager, of the saloon. The man stood maybe two inches less than Mark, but looked like he would weigh a mite heavier, for although he had a spread to his shoulders he did not taper down to a lean waist. He wore expensive gambler style clothes, with just too much clashing color to them for Mark's taste. His face was florid, jovial looking, yet there seemed to be a hardness under it, a kind of cold calculation as if the man would enjoy a good laugh only should it pay him to make it. To Mark's eyes the man looked like a hard-case who had gradually run to fat but who could still handle himself in a brawl.

"Howdy," Mark replied. The man looked too much like a trail-end town joint owner for Mark to take to him, but he felt he would lose nothing by being sociable.

"You're new around here," the man went on.

Even while he spoke the man's eyes studied Mark from head to foot, pricing his clothing and noting the matched guns in the hand-carved holsters of the gun-belt. Mark could almost guess what the man thought. That Mark was rich, a rancher's son maybe, possibly the owner of his own spread. A man who might have some influence or powerful backing, and a man who had it paid a saloonkeeper to know.

"I'm not old around anyplace," drawled Mark.

The man bellowed out a real professional hand-shaker's gust of laughter, the kind which could be turned on even at a feeble witticism, should the maker of the joke be someone worth knowing.

"I'm Homer Trent," boomed the man, clearly having decided Mark suitable material for cultivation. "This's my place. Say, have a drink on the house."

"Take another beer," Mark replied. "Did you ride under Hood in the War?"

"Huh? – Oh, the name of the place. Nope, I didn't ride with him. But folks in town here think high of him. You ranching out this way?"

"Nope, not yet."

Before he spoke again Trent threw a look at the wall clock. Then he grinned and dropped his voice in a confidential whisper:

"Say, if you feel like some real sport go sit in on the big faro table over there. It'll be worth it."

"Will, huh?"

"Sure," grinned Trent. "I've got Poker Alice and Madam Moustache here and they both of them expect to be dealing the big table for me."

Saying that Trent stood back a pace and grinned

broadly, awaiting Mark's reaction to his words. The names did not pass over Mark's head, for he had heard them many times. Poker Alice and Madam Moustache had something of a name in western saloon circles. They were lady gamblers and almost unique. True there had been and probably still were saloongirls who handled a wheel-of-fortune, or maybe turned the cards at a vingt-un layout to draw in customers. But they offered only a come-on for the gullible and woman hungry male customers and remained no more than saloongirls throughout. Poker Alice and Madam Moustache were different. They did not work as saloongirls, but as professional dealers, highly skilled at their work and offered nothing more than a male gambler would under the same circumstances.

While Mark could see the reason for hiring such talent to deal faro, he could not see why Trent took on both women. Mark's eyes went to the big table at which Trent pointed. This would be the house's big game, the no-limit table where the high stake players gathered and as such be the place of honor in the professional dealer's eyes. Both Poker Alice and Madam Moustache had handled such a table before and could do so with ease, so Mark wondered which of them would receive the honor, or if there were two high stake tables. His glance around the room saw two other tiger decorated faro lay-outs, but each bore a stakes sign restricting the level of betting.

"Ah!" Trent said eagerly. "Here comes Poker Alice."

Mark turned to look in the direction which Trent stared. The man looked up at the stair which led to the upstairs balcony and rooms. The woman he had seen at the hotel came down the stairs slowly, drawing every eye to her. He could now see what she wore under her cloak and as he perceived that now discarded cloak concealed a figure well worth a second, third and as many other glances as a man could spare at it.

She wore a white dress which would not have been out of place at a high class New Orleans ball and which showed off her rich figure to perfection. Maybe Poker Alice stood just a little mite taller than most men would call ideal, but she was not skinny, her figure seemed to be just right.

Ignoring the envious glares of the saloongirls and the frank, pop-eyed staring of the customers, Poker Alice reached the foot of the stairs and swept majestically towards the faro table.

Excitedly Trent jabbed Mark hard in the ribs with his elbow and was lucky not to get tossed over the bar for doing it. If he noticed Mark's angry scowl he ignored it in his excitement as he pointed to the other side of the room and whispered. "Look!"

Holding back his first instinct to remove Trent forcibly, Mark looked to where another woman also made her way across the room towards the main faro table. Mark studied her and decided that a man would be hard put to find two more beautiful women than the pair who converged on the dealer's seat. Yet they were as unalike as night and day. The other woman had none of Poker Alice's calm, regal detachment and cold aloofness. Her raven-black hair hung shoulder long and framed an olive skinned, beautiful face which radiated charm, vivacious love of life, merriment and a bold challenge. In height she stood maybe two inches shorter than the English woman, yet seemed much smaller. Her figure was ripe, richly curved, not quite plump but enough to give a man a good handful happen he took a chance and grabbed. Where Alice wore a sedate gown of white, cut in the latest eastern mode, the other girl had on a flame colored dress which clung almost like a second skin to her and had a slit from hem to well above the knee through which a black stockinged, plump and inviting leg peaked and disappeared at each step.

One thing Mark noticed, neither woman had long nails, or wore rings. He knew why. Players who knew their business objected to joining a game where the dealer's nails were long enough to mark the cards during play, or who wore rings in which tiny "shiner" mirrors might be concealed wherewith to see the value of each card dealt.

A second thing also struck Mark and he took his eyes from the two women to turn to Trent who stood watching in an expectant manner.

"Looks like they both figure to run the big table for you," he said.

"That's right, they do."

"That could mean trouble."

Trent grinned a conspiring grin as if letting Mark be a party to his secret plans. He dropped his voice to a confidential whisper and said:

"If there ain't trouble we'll all be disappointed."

"How do you mean?" growled Mark.

"Why'd you reckon I got 'em both here and started them on the same day, at the same time?" Trent replied. "There should be a better brawl than the battle at Bearcat Annie's."

It did not take Mark five seconds to see what Trent meant. The saloonkeeper had brought together the west's two foremost lady gamblers in the hope they would tangle in a hair-yanking brawl. He did not need both of them and would most likely let the winner stay on while the loser would have to leave town.

In this plan Trent showed a thorough working knowledge of the saloon business. Nothing could better bring a saloon to the notice of the public than a fight between persons of note. If two gunmen locked horns, especially two top name men, in a saloon, that saloon's reputation would be enhanced and people come to see the place where it happened. A remembered fight between two well-known females had the same effect. Bearcat Annie's saloon in Quiet Town, although under new management, still drew trade on the strength of the fight which had been fought in it and already customers made the pilgrimage to Tennyson to drink in Madam Bulldog's saloon where the girls recounted blow by blow descriptions of their boss' fight with Calamity Jane.

With this in mind Trent had set about building a legend about his place. He did not leave the meeting and fight to chance, but brought in the two lady gamblers, set them up and stood back hoping for the best, knowing full well that both had a lot of pride in their ability at handling a big stake faro game.

By now the women were almost at the table and Mark gave a low, angry growl. Trent looked at the big Texan and saw he did not give the hoped for reaction. With a shrewd knowledge of men, Trent could see that Mark did not approve of his idea and might even now spoil it, for Mark looked big enough to go against popular opinion and tough enough to back his actions. So Trent turned away and gave a sign which brought two of his bouncers to his side. He did not need to speak, a nod and a wink sent the two big, burly men to flank Mark, one on either side. If Mark noticed the arrival he did not connect it with anything to do with what Trent said, for his full attention stayed on the table and the two women. If he could prevent it he did not intend the fight to take place.

Not that Mark was a spoilsport in any way. He had the typical western sense of humor and liked the entertainment to be gamey and unrefined. If the two women tangled in the normal course of events Mark would not have objected and would have been quite willing to sit back and enjoy the fight, for he did not worry about the moral objections to letting a pair of women fight. What Mark did object to was that the women had been tricked into coming to Culver Creek for the sole purpose of causing trouble between them for the enrichment of the saloonkeeper. He aimed to walk across the room and stop the fight before it started.

Now would be the time to move, for already Poker Alice had reached the dealer's chair. Trent glanced at his bouncers and nodded. It cost him a considerable sum of money to bring the two women together and he did not intend allowing a chance passing stranger, even one who showed signs of being wealthy, to interfere.

"One moment, *mademoiselle*!" said a voice as Poker Alice was about to draw out the dealer's chair, a soft, provocative woman's voice which brought Alice's attention to the speaker.

She turned and faced the black haired beauty, looked her up and down, then replied, "Well?"

"This is my table," said Eleonore Dumont, better known as Madame Moustache, her accents those of a New Orleans French Creole of good birth and with a trace of an accent.

"I'm afraid it *was* your table," Alice replied. "I was brought in to take over the game."

"You!" Eleonore gasped. "Surely know that Madam Moustache, which is me, always runs the big table in any house which hires me."

"I'm afraid I've never heard of Madam Moustache," sniffed Alice calmly. "But I happen to be Poker Alice. Now trot along like a good little girl and I'm sure Mr. Trent will let you turn his wheel-of-fortune."

Poker Alice had told a lie when she said she had never heard of Madam Moustache and Eleonore acted ignorant of who the blonde girl might be. They had their pride and were deadly rivals although they had never run across each other before. Neither was the type to become involved in unseemly brawls, but they also both knew how to take care of themselves when a quarrel was forced on to them by jealous girls. Also neither would back down, give way to her rival at the big-game table.

"Take your hand off the chair!" Alice ordered, seeing every eye on her and Eleonore, reading the expectancy in their gaze. She did not wish to be put into the indignity of fighting, but would not back down.

"Make me!" hissed Eleonore, who did not really want to fight but also would not give way.

With an annoyed frown Alice released the back of the chair. Instantly Eleonore moved. Her right arm swung around to land on Alice's cheek in a flat-handed slap which snapped the blonde's head across to her lashing left palm causing Alice to take a hurried pace to the rear. Alice rocked under the impact of the slaps and Eleonore waited, tense as an alley-cat. Usually such a savage and rapid attack resulted in the one receiving it bursting into tears and taking a hurried departure. Only this time Eleonore did not face a saloongirl.

After catching her balance Alice swung a fist, not a slap, in return. Her knuckles cracked against the side of Eleonore's cheek and the Creole beauty went backwards on her heels, arms flailing to prevent herself from falling.

She spat out a mouthful of rapid French curses then sprang forward like a wildcat. Alice attacked at the same instant and the two women seemed to meet in mid-air. Hands dug into hair, tugging and yanking, or flailed in wild slaps and punches while feet lashed and kicked just as wildly. Clinging to each other and swinging wildly the two women crashed to the floor and rolled over and over, Alice's pale skin making a contrast to the tan of the Creole Girl.

As soon as the fight started almost everybody in the room either stood up and gathered around to get a better view, or climbed on chairs, tables, anywhere that offered them a vantage point over the heads of the standing crowd. The men yelled their encouragement but the saloongirls gathered in a sullen group and scowled at Alice and Eleonore, who they regarded as interlopers, for taking the center of attraction away from them.

At the bar, as soon as the two women met, Mark felt hands clamp on both his arms, strong and powerful hands which knew their business.

"Let's go easy, *hombre*!" a growling voice whispered in his ear and the two bouncers started walking him towards the door. "Just keep on going, boyo, and you won't get hurt."

They took five steps forward. To one side the squeals, gasps and yelps of the two fighting women became almost drowned by the excited shouts of the crowd and the calls of the gamblers offering to take bets on the winner. Mark decided he had gone as far as he aimed to go.

Instantly the two men hustling him towards the door came to a halt as Mark dug his heels in. Up until that moment the bouncers had been fooled and lulled into a sense of false security by Mark's appearance. They regarded him as a rich dandy, which he was due to an aunt leaving her considerable fortune to him in her will, and easy meat, which he most certainly was not. So the sudden halt took them both by surprise for it felt as if they had run into a brick wall.

Before either man could make up his mind what to do, the one at the right felt himself lifted from the floor. It took him completely by surprise when he felt his two hundred and thirty pounds of bone and muscle hefted up into the air, which delayed his reactions.

With a sudden surge of power Mark flung the right hand bouncer from him like a hound-dog shaking off a fly. The startled bouncer let out a howl and went head first across the room to smash into a table on which stood several soldiers all eagerly watching the fighting girls. With a crash the table went over and half a dozen soldiers pitched all ways, bellowing out curses and landing on other spectators as they went down. Men cursed, yelled and tempers boiled, so it did not help matters that the bartender should be a man with a bad reputation amongst soldiers due to some rough handling he had handed out. Fists started flying and a general brawl developed rapidly.

At the same moment that he flung aside the first man

Mark brought the other around with a jerk of his left arm. Before the bouncer could release his hold, Mark's right fist rammed into his stomach with a thud like a bass drum's stick striking the skin of the drum. The bouncer let out a startled and agonized gurgle, lost his hold on Mark's left arm and folded hands over his stomach as he doubled over. Mark shot down a hand, gripped the bouncer by the shirt collar and heaved, sending him shooting off after his pard into the tangle of spectators.

Next moment almost every man in the place became involved in the general brawl as the fight spread like stone-raised ripples crossing the surface of a pool. A waiter sprang at Mark, swinging up his heavy tray and launching a blow at the big Texan's head. Mark side-stepped, shot out his hands, gripped the tray, plucking it from the man's grasp and applying it with some force to its owner's head, sending him staggering dazedly off towards a group of fighting men. One of them turned on him and knocked him down. Mark heard Trent's enraged bellows and saw the saloonkeeper still stood at the bar. A chair hissed through the air and Trent ducked, allowing it to smash into the big mirror behind the bar. At that moment a cowhand flung himself at Mark who back-handed him aside then started towards the door. This proved to be a slow process, for the fight had now become general and not one between the various fractions in the saloon. It was now a case of at-tack the nearest person and hope not to get jumped by somebody else while doing it.

After thrashing over and over on the floor, Poker Alice and Madame Moustache made their feet, still holding hair with one hand and using the other to slap, push, punch and pull. They staggered clear of the fighting men and towards the foot of the stairs where the saloongirls stood screeching curses, yelling wild en-couragement or watching; their retreat to the bedrooms remained open in case a hurried departure should become necessary.

One of the girls let out an angry yell and charged forward, making for the two fighting women. Why she decided to cut in even she probably could not say. It might have been excitement, a desire to get in on the act. It could even have been through annoyance; she had been on the verge of persuading a gullible young cowhand to give her money for a stageline ticket to visit her (non-existent) sick mother in Arkansas when the fight started and caused him to lose interest. Whatever the motive, she rushed forward, dug two hands into Eleonore's long, though now considerably ruffled and untidy, black hair and started to pull hard.

The attack from behind came as a complete surprise and Eleonore gave out a squeal like a tail-stomped cougar. She lost her hold of Alice and was dragged clear of the dishevelled blonde. Alice might have been grateful for the help, but did not get a chance to show it, for a second girl darted from the stairs, thrusting Eleonore and her attacker aside. She delivered a slap to Alice's face, hard enough to leave fingermarks on her cheek. With a squeal Alice staggered back a couple of paces. She caught her balance, shot out her left hand to the girl's shoulder, measuring her up. Then the right hand swung around, clenched into a hard little fist. The saloongirl walked into the punch and shot backwards amongst her friends as they advanced to lend a hand. They all went down in a pile and forgot about Alice and Eleonore as various feuds came to a head in wild fighting among themselves.

Twisting and squealing, Eleonore struggled to free herself from the girl behind her but could not. However, Alice, having dealt with her assailant, turned to renew hostilities with her business rival. She sprang forward and sportingly landed a punch on the saloongirl, sending her reeling and sprawling back into her friends, where she became involved in a fight of her own.

To show her gratitude Eleonore lowered her head and butted into Alice, ramming her backwards into the main brawl where they tangled and fought on amongst the flailing fists and flying chairs.

Mark heard a bellow of rage and from the corner of his eye saw the first bouncer he had tossed aside coming at him in a low crouching charge, arms widespread to clamp around Mark. Only at the last moment Mark side-stepped and his foot raised to drive behind the man's rump and send him hurtling into the side wall where he slid down and lay still. Another man sprang at Mark, lifting a chair, but Mark bent, stepped forward, caught his attacker around the knees, then straightened to pitch him on to a soldier who had been moving in for an attack from the rear.

"Get the marshal!" Trent howled. "Get the shotgun from under the bar!"

Neither request had the slightest result, everybody in the room being far too busy defending themselves from a variety of assaults, even the bartenders, who might have handed over the shotgun from beneath the counter, had deserted the sober side of the bar to help out in the general tangle.

After howling out his request again Trent realized his position and started to lean over the counter. His hands almost closed on the butt of the shotgun when a hand grabbed his coat, hauled him off and sent him sprawling back into the fight where another fist smashed into the side of his jaw and knocked him further from the bar and his weapon.

By that time Mark had almost reached the doors, being driven aside so he now stood by the side wall. A pretty red-headed girl who had lost her frock and gained what looked like it would be a glorious mouse under her left eye emerged from the center of a knot of fighting men in which she had been tangled. She held a bottle gripped by the neck and clearly meant to use it as a club against somebody. Her eyes settled on Mark first and she rushed at him. The bottle swung up and slapped her wrist into his palm. He hooked his other arm around her waist, pulled her to him and kissed her hard. The girl's free hand clawed wildly at Mark's shoulder, let loose then tightened again. The fingers holding the bottle relaxed, allowing it to fall unheeded to the floor. He released the girl and she staggered back, glassy-eyed, to bump into a cowhand who turned and swung a fist which knocked the girl down even before he realized who he struck at. Mark flattened the cowhand as a matter of principle. He then looked around the room to try and locate Poker Alice and Madam Moustache, but among that seething, struggling crowd, he could not locate the two women.

For their part Alice and Eleonore went at it like a pair of Kilkenny cats. They had no fighting skill and their tactics were pure woman. They pushed, shoved, slapped and kicked at each other, climbing over, dodging behind or crawling between other fighters to get at each other. A man on his knees grabbed Alice around the waist. She felt her frock ripping but before she could escape or do anything about it Eleonore jumped in and launched a kick which a *savate* fighter might have envied. Her shoe caught the man under the jaw and landed hard enough to both make him release his hold and cause him to lose interest in the proceedings. Alice showed her appreciation for the help by landing a couple of explosive slaps across Eleonore's bare shoulders, then they closed with each other again. By now they were at the far side of the room but still going at it with all they had.

Trent was raging in fury as he saw his saloon being wrecked before his eyes. His careful plan for a bit of free advertisement had gone sadly astray. Instead of a cat-fight between the two women he had a brawl which saw his fixtures being shattered and his staff damaged.

A bunch of fighting men landed on the big-stake faro table which crumpled and collapsed under them. The wheel-of-fortune rocked from its place on the wall and broke on the floor. Trent saw this happen, then through a gap in the crowd, saw Alice and Eleonore. In his fury he blamed everything that was happening upon the two women and swore they would pay for every bit of the damage they caused.

He avoided a soldier's attack and smashed a blow at the side of the man's head, felling him. With a snarl Trent thrust himself forward and headed towards the two women, swinging a fist or a kick at anyone who crossed his path and without regard for sex or position in life. Coming on to the two women who he blamed for his troubles Trent let out a bellow of rage and stamped towards them, grabbing them by the arms.

It proved to be the wrong thing to do. With screeches which sounded like a pair of she-bobcats defending their young, the two women turned on Trent. His hair was yanked out in chunks, his shins hacked by wild lashing feet. Trent's enraged bellows changed to yells of pain. He grabbed the two women around their waists and tried to crush them to him as they all staggered backwards.

A flying chair just missed Trent and the girls, which proved to be fortunate for them as it shattered the big front window at which they headed. Tight and entwined as a king snake killing a diamondback rattler, the three went into the window frame and crashed through on to the street below, landing amongst the broken glass, luckily without cutting themselves. The force of the landing winded the two girls and they rolled from the dazed Trent's arms, laying on the sidewalk.

Trent rolled to his hands and knees, shaking his head and spitting out lurid curses. A large crowd had gathered before his place to see the fun, but the marshal had not made a show of himself yet. This did not surprise Trent who knew the marshal held his post by means of his lax law enforcement rather than by zeal and vigor in the line of duty. Having heard of the fight, Trent did not doubt that the marshal would be waiting for things to cool down before arriving and trying to do anything about breaking it up.

Forcing himself to his feet Trent looked down at the two exhausted women. His never amiable temper burst in full flood upon them, blaming them for everything which happened inside his place since their arrival.

"You lousy calico cats!" he screamed, no other word could describe the sounds he made. "I'll teach you to have my place wrecked. I'll have the pair of you in jail and working for me until you've paid back every cent of the damage that's been done!"

At that moment the other front window smashed outwards as a table sailed through it. Thinking of the cost of those big windows, Trent bellowed in rage and drew back his foot meaning to sink it into Poker Alice's unprotected ribs.

Somebody landed a punch on Mark Counter's jaw and sent the big Texan sprawling through the batwing doors. Mark never did learn who hit him, all he knew was that whoever did it packed a real good punch. It propelled Mark through the batwing doors and into the hitching rail. Catching the upright support Mark stopped himself going flying into the street. He put a hand to his jaw and winced, that *hombre* inside landed a punch like his *amigo* Dusty Fog. For a moment Mark thought of going back and trying conclusions with the man who handled such a good punch. Then he saw something which drove all such thoughts from his head.

The shattering of the first window brought his attention to it so he saw Trent and the girl make their hurried departure through the broken frame. He also saw Trent rise and heard the threats uttered.

Not until Trent started to draw back his foot and kick Alice did Mark move. But when he moved – man he moved fast.

With long strides Mark shot along the sidewalk and reached Trent even before the saloonkeeper could draw

back his foot. Mark's left hand shot out and caught
Trent's arm. The saloonkeeper let out a low snarl and
started to turn, throwing a punch. Faster than Trent
moved, Mark deflected the blow over his head and then
shot out a bunched fist which carried all his weight
behind it. Trent's head snapped back and he reeled into
the window, performed a neat somersault back over the
low edge and disappeared from sight.

Mark looked down at the girls. He guessed from the
fact that the town law had not arrived to help quell the
disturbance what sort of marshal he could expect. The
owner of a fine, or what had been a fine, saloon would
undoubtedly exert some considerable pull over such a
lawman and could arrange that Alice and Madam
Moustache be jailed then fix such a heavy fine on them
that they would virtually be his slaves until they paid it
off.

This did not meet with Mark's ideas of the fitness of
things. The two women came in all good faith to deal
faro for Trent and under the agreement that each of
them would run his big stake game. Either woman
would have fulfilled her side of the bargain and brought
in a good return for her cut in the game. Only Trent
would not be content with that. He wanted to use the
reputations of Poker Alice and Madam Moustache to
glorify his place, by setting them at each other's throats.
So Mark did not see why either of them should suffer.

He bent and scooped one girl up under each arm,
holding them around the waist and letting head and feet
dangle. They hung there limp and unresisting as he
headed around the side of the saloon. The watching
crowd gave him a warm cheer of approval but none
tried to interfere with him. In that they showed
prudence, for Mark was in no mood to be trifled with.
Before anybody could think of following Mark and
discover what he aimed to do with the two girls, a bunch
of screaming, fighting women burst through the saloon
doors and drew the crowd's attention to them.

Carrying his limp bundles, Mark headed for the hotel's stable. He doubted if a night's rest would cool Trent's desire for revenge and so the only thing to do would be to get the two women out of town and away from his sphere of influence.

The stable looked deserted when Mark entered. However, as he dumped his load into the straw of an empty stall Mark heard a footstep and turned to find the old-timer he spoke with earlier had come from his office at the far end.

"Now that's what I call a couple of trophies," he cackled, throwing a glance at the two girls.

"A man'd say you called it right," agreed Mark, then pointed to Alice. "This the one who brought that fancy rig in?"

"That's her. What happened?"

"Trent started a tangle between her and the other gal."

The old man spat. "That'd be his mark all right."

"I've got to get them both out of town," Mark went on, seeing the man did not appear to hold the saloon-keeper in very high esteem. "The saloon got wrecked a lil mite."

"Sounded that way."

"Hitch the team while I go collect my gear from the hotel."

"Why, sure, go right ahead."

Mark threw a glance at the girls, seeing they had recovered enough to shove themselves up on their hands while still laying flopped out in the straw. Then he left the stable and headed to the hotel while the old man started to lead out the harness horses.

Clearly the hotel staff and guests had left to see the fight at the saloon, for he could see no sign of anybody. The reception desk was deserted and Mark looked at the register, hoping to locate Madam Moustache's room. He could neither find that name, nor one which sounded even remotely French, so concluded, correctly, she must be staying at some other hotel. There would be no time to try and find it and then collect Madam's belongings, so Mark decided he must abandon them until such time as they could be safely collected.

From his own room he gathered his bedroll and Winchester and, having taken her key as well as his own, Mark went across to Poker Alice's room and entered. He found that apart from one case she had brought little or nothing with her. With all the speed he could manage Mark stuffed Alice's belongings into the case, fastened it and left the room, locking the door.

By the time he reached the stables he found the hitching of the team to be going on. He also found that Poker Alice and Madam Moustache had recovered enough to be fighting with each other again. Muffled screams, squeals and scuffling noises came from the stall and the old-timer threw a look towards it.

"Yes, sir," he said. "A couple of real trophies. I sure admire you all for trying to take them on the hoof."

Mark looked at the stall where four legs, each encased in a tattered black silk stocking and showing an expanse of white flesh slashed with black suspender above them, thrashed and waved as the struggling girls rolled over and over. The old man took a look also, for either pair of legs was neat enough to attract attention. He could not take much time to admire the view, for Mark wanted to leave town as soon as possible.

"Saddle your hoss, friend," the old-timer suggested. "Then if I need help you can give it to me."

This struck Mark as being the best idea, so he followed the old man's instructions. By the time he had the bloodbay saddled and bridled, he saw the old man did not need his help. Mark lashed his bedroll into place and thrust the Winchester into the saddleboot. He secured the horse's reins to the rear of the carriage and turned to the business of separating the women without getting hand-scalped in the process.

At that moment they both reared up, then dragged

themselves to their feet. Although on the last verge of exhaustion they still clung to each other. During the brawl in the straw Alice had lost her skirt. Now they rose and Eleonore's dress at last gave up the uneven struggle and peeled from her, leaving her exposed in a set of the latest fashion, very brief, black lace underwear. Even this did nothing to make them break up their fight.

Without a thought, though with a good look, at how the two women were now attired, Mark stepped forward. He used a tactic a female deputy in Quiet Town demonstrated on several occasions as being best for such a situation. Shooting out his hands he gripped each woman by the scruff of her neck, drew them apart, then brought their heads together with a thud. Alice and Eleonore went limp and he let them fall into the straw. They would not be causing him any trouble for a spell.

"I sure likes to see a chivalrous southern gent," grinned the old-timer who had finished hitching the team and was securing Alice's bag on top of the trunk.

"And me," grinned Mark. "Last one I saw who tried to split apart a pair of tangling females ended up as a bald-headed chivalrous southern gent and I'm too handsome to want to be bald."

He handed the old man a twenty-dollar gold piece and then lifted first Alice and then Eleonore into the carriage, putting them in the rear covered seat and draping them over with the rug which had been curled on the seat. Swinging up on to the driving seat, Mark took up the reins and whip. He gave the old-timer a cheery salute and sent the horses out into the night, the bloodbay following on their heels.

On leaving Culver Creek behind him Mark gave thought to getting away from possible pursuit. He knew roughly the direction in which to head for Holbrock City and could most likely follow this trail to it. But then men who Trent would send after the girls could just as easily follow the road and make better time.

With this thought in mind Mark swung the team from the trail and headed out across the range. He headed at right angles to the trail for a mile, then turned the team in the direction he wished to go. Behind him he could hear gasps as the carriage bounced over the rough ground but kept his full attention on steering the team. He wanted to put as many miles as he could between himself and Culver City before finding a camp site for the night.

Not until Culver City lay a good six miles behind them did Mark draw rein. He located a small stream and followed its banks until he found a wood in which he could hide the wagon from chance passers. For the first time he looked around at his passengers. They were hanging on to each other's neck for all the world like two sleeping babies, although Mark could never remember seeing two babies at which he would rather look. Apparently they had been so exhausted that when they recovered from his pacifying methods they must have drifted off into sleep.

Poker Alice stirred, then opened her eyes. She stared at Mark for a moment and groaned, "Where am I?"

"Sorry I had to bounce you about, ma'am," Mark replied. "It was that or stay on the trail and likely wind you both up back in the Culver City jail."

For the first time Alice seemed to notice how she was dressed, for the rug had slipped down from them. She gave a gasp, bent and dragged the covering back up over herself, although only partially over Madam Moustache who groaned and opened her eyes.

"What is happening?" she asked. "Where – wha—"

At that moment Alice turned and stared at her rival. Recognition was mutual and instantaneous. However, Alice made no move to resume hostilities with Eleonore. Her hand dropped under the rug and to the edge of the seat. From where it lay hidden, she drew a Remington Double Derringer and lined it on Mark.

"I think you owe us an explanation," she said coolly.

"You'll find another Derringer at the edge of your seat, Madam, if you know how to use one."

"I never needed one to deal with a man before," Eleonore replied, then for the first time she appeared to become aware of the scanty nature of her attire. "My dress!" she wailed.

"You left it in the stable back at Culver City," Mark told her, then looked at the four .41 calibre barrels which lined on him, for Eleonore also produced a Derringer and handled it in a manner which showed she, like Alice, knew which end the bullet emerged.

He explained quickly what had happened, both Trent's plan for bringing them together and his threat at the end. They listened, but neither let their gun barrels waver any.

"I see," Alice said when Mark finished speaking and she had thought over his statements. "May I ask who you are?"

"The name's Mark Counter and I'd sure admire to see those guns pointed some other place. Happen I'd felt that way earlier I could have done what I wanted afore either of you knowed what was coming off."

"You've a point there," Eleonore replied. "I think we can trust you."

"I wouldn't want to accept your judgment on anything, darling," Alice stated. "But this time I believe you're right."

They both tucked the Derringers out of sight once more and Mark waved a hand to the team.

"I'll tend to the horses," he told them. "Then I reckon I'd best throw some wood up and start a fire. I've some air-tights in my war bag, if one of you ladies can do the cooking."

"I think an improvement in dress is called for," Alice remarked.

The words brought a wail from Eleonore. "My clothes! I haven't anything here to put on."

"That's deucedly awkward," purred Alice. "I took

the precaution of leaving my trunk on my carriage. And our gallant rescuer appears to have brought my bag from the hotel too."

"Sure," Mark agreed, then looked at Eleonore. "I'd've brought your gear, but I couldn't find if you had a room at the hotel."

"I didn't. I was staying at the other hotel. I always leave my bag at the stage depot for the first two days, with word that if I have to leave town in a hurry they are to send it on to some other place."

"Do you often have to leave town in a hurry?" Alice asked.

"Not often. I am a square gambler, as I have always heard you are," Eleonore answered in an angry voice. "But you know how the goody-goodies and do-gooders are in some towns. 'A woman gambler? Tut, tut! How terrible. We can't have her besmirching the morals of our fair city.' You know what I mean."

Alice started to laugh. Whatever else she might be Eleonore could certainly make her voice sound just like a small town do-gooder denouncing the evils of a woman gambler, or any other kind of sin.

"I know," she agreed. "A few weeks ago I used to have a maid, but she married a cowhand. I've two of her uniforms at the bottom of my trunk. At least they'll serve until you can collect your belongings from wherever you sent them – if you can get into them, you are somewhat fatter than the girl."

"FATTER!" squealed Eleonore, raising her fists and then bursting into a string of French Creole curses.

"Now hold it, girls!" Mark put in before either could make a move to resume physical hostilities. "Was I you I'd leave off the hair-yanking until you get out of that carriage. Happen the team spooks and run, you'll be in bad . . ."

His words calmed the girls down enough to stop an immediate attack. Eleonore looked at Alice and saw the twinkle in the English girl's eyes. Her own volatile nature warmed immediately and she burst into a merry laugh.

"I've always found men prefer a woman with something they can get their hands on," she stated. "Of course you can't help being skinny. I suppose you never win enough gambling to afford a decent meal."

"*Touché!*" smiled Alice.

"I'll make a fire," Mark drawled, "You can get into something warmer while I'm gathering the wood."

When he returned from searching amongst the trees for dry wood Mark found Alice wearing a long housecoat while Eleonore had the carriage rug wrapped around her and looked in danger of losing it at any moment. Alice clearly thought an explanation for the lack of clothes to be in order, for she turned to Mark as he started to light the fire.

"We couldn't see to unpack the trunk, so we're doing the best we can."

With the fire lit Mark went to take care of the horses. The two women came to lend a hand, but after she had lost the blanket twice Eleonore decided she would do better to attend to building the fire up. She left Mark and Alice to unhitch and hobble the team horses and raised a comforting blaze. Then while Alice opened her trunk, Mark cared for his big stallion, removing its saddle and bridle and letting it free to graze, knowing it would not stray far.

"It's no good," Alice remarked. "I've got my bedroll out, but I can't find our clothes. I suggest we turn in after a cup of coffee and I'll find the dresses in the morning."

Clearly Alice had camped out at nights before, for she carried a coffeepot, skillet and the necessities of life in two sacks in her trunk, along with a western style bedroll.

For the first time, when they all gathered about the fire to drink the coffee, Mark found a chance of looking the girls over. Their hair looked tangled and untidy and their faces and shoulders were dirty, bruised, yet neither showed too much sign of the fight. Possibly Eleonore would have a black eye in the morning but nothing more, for the fight had been more hair yanking, slapping and pushing than fist swinging.

"I hope I don't look as big a mess as you do," Alice remarked to Eleonore, reading Mark's thoughts from his glance.

"It is nothing that water and a comb will not cure," Eleonore replied.

"Where are you ladies going to sleep?" Mark asked.

"I'll bed down under the carriage as I usually do," Alice replied. "Madam here can sleep on the back seat if we loan her some of our bedding."

So it was arranged, Mark settled down after he had seen the two women rolled in the blankets. Time passed and the fire died down. A soft footfall woke Mark and he looked up to find Eleonore standing by his bed, the rug draped scantily about her.

"I couldn't sleep, Mark," she said and sat down beside him.

"Thought you would be able to after that shindig back at the saloon," he replied with a grin.

Throwing a glance at where Alice's shape could be seen under the carriage Eleonore gave a laugh.

"That is a tough girl, my Mark," she sighed. "What a brawl."

"Sure was, Madam."

She nestled closer to him and he felt that the rug had slipped from her body. Under the lace her body was warm and inviting.

"Don't call me Madam," she said. "I am Eleonore Dumont. Would you like to hear how I came by the Madam Moustache name?"

"Why sure."

"It is chilly, can't we make ourselves more comfortable as we talk?"

"Anything you say," Mark replied.

They stretched out side by side and he drew the blankets and suggans over them, then slipped an arm under her neck while her arms entwined with his.

Eleonore Dumont had been born to a middle class French Creole family but grew with the wanderlust in her feet. She left home to travel with a small show which presented plays like East Lynne to such backwood villages as they came across in their travels. One member of the show had been a retired Mississippi riverboat gambler and he taught the girl all he knew about the mysteries of gambling. She proved to be a willing learner and when the show finally broke up, as such shows always did, Eleonore found herself stranded in Wichita. There were few things a young woman might do to earn a living in the west, but none of them appealed to Eleonore. At last she decided to put her gambling knowledge to a test. Here she ran into her first snag. The saloons allowed women inside only as employees and a few gambling houses allowed women at all, none allowed them in the capacity of player.

In desperation Eleonore borrowed a man's suit from the belongings of the disbanded company of actors, also a false moustache. In this she entered Bailey's gambling house. Her luck stood fair and she brought her twenty dollar stake to two hundred on the faro layout, then joined a poker game. Once more the gods of chance smiled on their daughter and she cleaned out the players, winning over two thousand dollars. All this was possible only because Bailey did not believe in wasting money and had few lights except those fixed to illuminate the playing surface of his tables. In fact Eleonore might have taken her winnings and escaped undetected had not a sneeze blown her moustache on to the table.

At first Bailey had been furious when he found a woman not only entered his place but cleaned out a table. However, he saw the humorous side of it. He also saw the attraction Eleonore would offer to him. She started work two nights later, as a dealer at the faro layout. The story of how she came to get the job passed around and men crowded in to see Madame Moustache, the lady gambler. From that day, five years before, Eleonore had never looked back. She travelled considerably and as Madame Moustache became well known.

That then was the story of Madam Moustache – but Mark Counter did not hear it until the following day. After all the night was passing and it seemed foolish to waste time in talking.

At dawn Alice awoke to find Eleonore and Mark already up and about. Eleonore had already gathered wood and started a fire and now brewed coffee over it while Mark gathered in the horses.

"Good morning," Alice greeted. "Sorry I overslept."

"A woman of your age needs her beauty sleep, darling," replied Eleonore.

"Look," sighed Alice. "Let's call the whole thing off, shall we. I hate to have to start making catty answers before breakfast."

She unpacked her travelling clothes and the older of her maid's costumes after they had eaten the food Eleonore cooked up. Handing the outfit to the dark-haired girl Alice suggested they went to the river, washed and changed.

Half an hour passed and the two women returned. The maid's clothes fitted Eleonore a trifle loosely and she frowned in a threatening manner at Mark who looked her over with a grin.

"Don't you dare say anything, my Mark!" she warned.

"All right. Where do you gals aim to go now?"

"Where are you going?" Alice asked.

"Holbrock. It's a fair sized town up north of here."

"That will do me, how about you, Madam?"

"I'll go along, we can chaperone each other," Eleonore answered. "I can telegraph Culver City and have them send my bags along."

With their destination decided Mark helped the two women to prepare for the journey. They kept on the range until noon, then swung back towards where Mark guessed the stage route to be. It said much for his plainsman's instinct that they found the trail, nothing more than the well worn ruts left by stages, horses and wagons travelling northwards to Holbrock.

They spent the night on the shores of a small lake. The proprieties were observed by them all. The girls bathed in the lake while Mark hunted for and shot a couple of cottontails for food, then they buried themselves in preparing a meal and let him have a swim. The proprieties were observed later too, for Eleonore went to bed on the seat of the carriage and most certainly was back there when Alice awoke the following morning.

Rather than push their horses too hard they spent a third night out on the range within four miles of Holbrock. They had supper and went to their respective beds as usual.

Mark heard the stealthy footsteps and felt the warm body wriggle alongside him and rolled over.

"Did I tell you how I became known as Poker Alice?"

The voice sounded just as cool, calm and collected as ever. It also came as quite a surprise to Mark, who had been expecting Eleonore. He could almost swear he heard a low chuckle from the carriage.

"Why'd it take you so long to decide to tell me?" he asked.

"My dear chap, one should never rush into – er, telling one's life story." Alice replied, slipping her hands around him and bringing her lips towards his face.

It appeared that Poker Alice had been born the only child to an eccentric younger son of a noble English house and that her mother died when she was just over a year old. Her father had been what she described as a bit of a masher, one of the men-about-town. Yet in his way he loved and cared for her and she grew up in an atmosphere of hunting, fishing, shooting as practised in England. She could ride a horse or handle a team and could use a shotgun very well. From one of her father's cronies, an earl whose family had lost its money in speculation which failed, she learned the secrets and arts of gambling.

On her father's death, riding to hounds (to disprove a doctor's theory that to do so with four broken ribs would prove dangerous), Alice took what she thought would be a trip around the world. In the United States she became fascinated with the gambling houses and with her calm assurance invaded the sacred domain of the male. Hoping to teach her a sharp lesson a group of poker players allowed her to sit in on their game. They taught her all right, to the tune of several thousand dollars of their money.

That night saw the birth of Poker Alice. She accepted the name they gave her and moved on. Seven years had passed and Alice's name was known over the west. Unlike Eleonore she rarely took the dealer's chair at a saloon faro layout, preferring to run her own poker game. She accepted Trent's offer to come to Culver Creek more to see a new section of country than because she wished to work for the man, meaning only to stay on for a couple of weeks, then if the town looked like it could accommodate it, start her own game. Her stay had been shorter than she expected.

However, Mark did not hear her story that night. What he did learn was that beyond the cool, calm and regally carried exterior Alice was all woman and did not come second even to the warm, volatile and vibrant Eleonore.

All in all Mark would not have minded if the journey

to Holbrock took another couple of days instead of finishing the following morning.

The carriage horses stepped out in a lively manner as if they knew they would be in a stall and getting grain fed when they reached the town. Mark rode his blood-bay alongside and listened to the story of Poker Alice's life, while Eleonore, with memories of telling her own life story still fresh in her memory, grinned broadly and winked at Mark.

Alice used the rest of the time until they came into sight of Holbrock to tell her life story. She stopped talking as the horses topped the last ridge and they saw the town at the foot of the slope.

From the look of things the town had grown considerably since the time, almost four years back, Dusty Fog and the Ysabel Kid paid it a brief but hectic visit.* Brenton Hunboldt's meat packing plant stood at the far side of the town, large and busy looking. The main street now looked more imposing and behind it ran other smaller streets leading to the houses of the workers at the plant and the subsidiary industries of the town.

On the side towards which Mark and his party now headed lay the homes of the richer members of the community, the influential citizens who controlled and ran the town. Showpiece of them all was Humboldt's house, a big, fine looking building of white stone and considerable elegance, with a large well cared for flower garden and lawns before it, a high iron railing fence around it, and a set of open wrought iron gates from which a gravel path swept in a curve to before the main entrance to the house.

Mark felt a little sad as he saw the gates ahead of him, soon he would be leaving the two girls to take on the boring task of being an honored guest at the wedding of two people he had never met and did not know. The

* Told in *The Half-Breed*.

two women would carry on into town, put up at the best hotel and make their plans for the future, most likely he would not see them again. Neither woman would be likely to open her game in town and probably did not intend to stay on any longer than it took to book a ride on the stage, or rest the carriage team. He grinned as he wondered what Humboldt would say if he rolled up and introduced Poker Alice and Madam Moustache as his friends. It might be amusing to see Humboldt's dilemma as he tried to get rid of the girls without offending Ole Devil Hardin's representative. Only the fact that such an action might embarrass the girls prevented Mark from carrying out his idea.

For their first arrival into Holbrock, Eleonore had made her long hair up in a bun and hidden it under a maid's cap. The dress she wore, especially when she sat on the driving box by Alice, hid and effectively disguised her figure so she looked little or nothing like the vivacious and beautiful Madam Moustache. Alice, in her severe travelling clothes and with her hair taken back tightly under a hat, did not look like the coolly beautiful woman who dealt cards in high stake poker games.

Being aware of the vindictive nature of Trent's kind they quite expected him to pull strings and have a warrant out for the arrest of Alice and Eleonore, then cause their return to Culver Creek where he might force them to pay for the damage his greed brought to his saloon. So the two women decided to adopt the simple disguise on their arrival in Holbrock and to see how the land lay before making a move.

Suddenly Eleonore drew her breath in with a hiss as she stared at two riders who turned from a side street ahead of them, glanced their way and started to ride along the street towards the town center, Mark studied the men and wondered what attracted Eleonore's attention to the men. To his eyes they, although wearing cowhand clothes, spelled hard-cases. They did not sit their horses or show that undefinable something which identified one cowhand to another. From the look of their low-hanging guns they were no more than a couple of toughs who would hire out fighting skill to the highest bidder. Yet Mark could almost swear he had seen some kind of a law badge on one's vest. Of course, their kind did find employment as deputies under a certain type of town marshal or county sheriff and Mark did not know what sort of law Holbrock might have.

"Those men!" Eleonore said, speaking quickly, but quietly. "The one on the right worked for Trent. I saw them together on the day I arrived and learned the man was a hired tough, supposedly a deputy, but really on Trent's payroll."

"You sure of that?" Mark asked, seeing the men talking together and taking surreptitious glances towards his party.

"Of course. I arrived in Culver Creek two days early, so as to look around and try to learn what sort of a place Trent ran. I saw that man and I rarely forget a face."

Mark could guess what the men were doing. They had seen him and noted the two women. In a moment they would ride back to start asking questions. So far they were not close enough to recognize either woman and make-up concealed such marks of the fight as remained. Possibly the two men did not believe Poker Alice and Madam Moustache would be riding side by side in a carriage and on amiable terms, but they might turn and come up to check.

"In there!" Mark snapped, indicating the gates leading to Humboldt's home.

To give her credit Alice reacted fast. She swung the head of her team towards the gates and Mark followed. He threw a glance towards the two men, seeing they had started to bring their horses around towards him. Mark followed the carriage and caught up alongside as it approached the front of the house.

Just as Alice halted her carriage before the imposing main entrance, the doors were flung open and Brenton Humboldt emerged in something of a hurry. He came to a halt at the sight of his visitors and a frown puckered his brow, for he did not know any of them.

"Mr. Humboldt?" Mark asked, although the big, pompous looking man in the expensive broadcloth suit fitted Dusty's description so well that he could be none other than Mr. Brenton Humboldt himself.

"That's correct."

Even as he made his reply Humboldt studied the party at his doors with some interest. He noted the team horses and the stylish, though trail-marked, carriage, both of which cost good money. Then he looked up at Alice. In some way she contrived to look far different from Poker Alice, yet still retained her air of refinement and gentility. Humboldt noted her expensive, though travel-stained clothes of impeccable good taste and her calm, dignified demeanor. He glanced at the obvious lady's maid seated by Alice, then finally studied Mark.

"I'm Mark Counter, from the OD Connected," Mark introduced. "Dusty couldn't get here, or the Kid, so I came."

A delighted beam crossed Humboldt's face, along with a flickering expression of relief, although Mark could not be sure whether this be caused by his arrival or the fact that the Ysabel Kid would not be on hand for the wedding.

Humboldt stepped forward with his hand extended. "Pleased to see you, Mr. Counter, or may I call you Mark? We were despairing of seeing anybody from the OD Connected, the wedding is tomorrow at eleven. Get down. I'll have one of the servants take care of your horse."

"I've got to take Lady Alice along to the hotel first," Mark answered. "She's travelling alone, except for her maid and I said I'd see her safe."

"Lady Alice?"

"Why sure. This is Lady Alice Hatton-Green. I met them out on the range this morning."

"I'm out here with pater," Alice put in, guessing what Mark had in mind and going along with it. "He's up-country on a big game hunt, but I decided I would come along and see one of your western towns."

"Pater?" asked the puzzled Humboldt.

"My father, Lord Hatton-Green. I suppose there is a hotel in town?"

"Well, yes, there is," agreed Humboldt. "But I'm sure we could put your Ladyship up here for a few days."

"I wouldn't wish to put you to any trouble," Alice replied and lifted her hands to start the team forward.

She hoped that Mark knew what he was doing, for the two men sat their horses across the street and in front of the gate, ready to halt the carriage and ask all kinds of inconvenient questions.

Mark knew Humboldt to be a snob of the first water and gambled on the man's willingness to be able to introduce a member of European nobility as a house guest when his friends came to his daughter's wedding. Mark knew Humboldt would never allow Poker Alice and Madam Moustache to enter his house, even to save them from trouble which was not of their making, so the big Texan used a trick. The lie had some slight truth in it. Alice did come from a noble British house but she could not claim to have Lady prefixed to her name.

"It will be no trouble," Humboldt put in hurriedly, reacting just as Mark guessed he would.

"I couldn't really accept your hospitality," Alice said and felt Eleonore dig a warning elbow into her ribs. However, Alice knew how to handle men of Brenton Humboldt's type and knew the more reluctant "Lady Alice Hatton-Green" appeared to be, the more eager would be his efforts to persuade her to stay.

"But I insist. My wife would never forgive me if I let

a Lad—you stay at the hotel. You must stay with us, we feel it is our duty to the good name of Texas to offer you our hospitality. Tell your maid to take your hand luggage to your room and I'll have your team attended to and your trunk brought up."

"Very well, thank you for the offer," Alice replied, giving in gracefully as if conferring a favor upon him. She looked towards Eleonore, "Fifi, bring the bag."

A hint of the red flush of annoyance crept to Eleonore's cheeks. Then she glanced at the gate and the two watching men. This was no time to object to a change of names.

"*Oui, oui,* your lady-*sheep!*" She answered, laying great emphasis on the last word although Humboldt thought it no more than a delightful French pronunciation.

Gallantly Humboldt helped Alice to alight from her carriage. He then turned and told the footman, who stood at the door watching everything with some pop-eyed amazement, to inform Mrs. Humboldt they had guests.

In the hall Mark and the girls watched with amusement as a rather annoyed-looking Mrs. Humboldt appeared from a room along the large hall which faced the main entrance. Humboldt bore down on her, leaving his guests, and began to whisper urgently. They could see the change in Mrs. Humboldt's attitude when she heard one of her guests was a Lady and the other the son of a very rich Texas rancher and a trusted member of the OD Connected ranch crew. This latter meant much less to Mrs. Humboldt than the fact that she had a chance to introduce a real British Lady to her friends.

Mrs. Humboldt bore down on the party. "James will show you to your room, Mr. Counter," she said. "And I will escort you, if I may, your ladyship. But I'm afraid that with the wedding tomorrow and everything we have no room to accommodate your maid. Perhaps she could stay at one of the hotels in town?"

"Hum!" Alice answered, seeing a chance to have some fun at Eleonore's expense. "I think not. I lost my last maid by letting her go out, she ran away with a cowhand."

"It's so difficult to get loyalty from the lower classes these days, isn't it?" agreed Mrs. Humboldt, throwing a glance at Eleonore who had to make an effort to stop landing her hostess a lusty kick in the bustle.

"Practically impossible," said Alice. "But I'll let Fifi stay in my room. Don't go to any trouble, just a few blankets will do and she can sleep on the floor. She's used to roughing it."

Only with an even greater effort did Eleonore restrain herself from planting a kick firmly on Alice's rear at the words. For the past few days she had tried to explain to Mark and Alice how she loved her creature comforts. Sleeping on a hard wooden floor did not come under the heading of creature comfort where she was concerned. However, through the still open front doors, she could see the two men sitting their horses and so kept a grip on Alice's bag and promised herself revenge at a later and more convenient date.

Not until alone with Alice in her room did Eleonore give vent to her feelings.

"*Fifi!*" she gasped. "She will be happy to sleep on the floor. I ought to—!"

"My good girl, that's no way for a maid to address her mistress," said Alice, trying hard to keep a straight face.

"Why you—!"

Not even Alice's years of gambling training could help her now and she began to smile, then laugh. For a moment Eleonore glared at Alice and contemplated all kinds of violence, then she, too, saw the funny side of things and also began to laugh.

"We're safe in here," Alice remarked. "That pair of hardcases are still out front, but they'll hear that Lady Alice Hatton-Green— I wonder where Mark dug that name up from, is a guest of Brenton Humboldt. They might be suspicious, but nobody in Holbrock's going to ask their leading citizen questions about his guest."

"They might, thinking to gain his approval by exposing us."

"Not if they know Humboldt. He'd rather have us stay here as Lady Alice and her maid than have it known he couldn't tell a real member of the aristocracy from a notorious gambling woman."

Thinking on it Eleonore agreed with Alice's judgment of Humboldt's character. One thing was certain. Humboldt would not thank the man who showed him up as a fool.

At that moment a knock came at the door and Eleonore opened it and proceeded to give her impression of how a French maid should act. Luckily the men gained their ideas of French maids from the same source as Eleonore, the theatre, so they expected her saucy winks and behavior.

"Breeng eet een here, *mon cherie*," she said to the burly man in the lead. "And be ver' careful or ze Lady Alice weel be mo' angry wiz me."

With that she ushered the two men into the room, chattering in the most atrocious broken English Alice could ever remember hearing as she had the trunk set down just where her mistress would like it.

After the men left, Alice turned to Eleonore and grinned broadly. "Where did you pick up that accent?" she asked.

"My mother was French," Eleonore answered, also grinning. "Don't you think I'd make a good maid?"

"To be frank, no."

"Or me. Look, I'd like to go into town and send a telegraph message to the Wells Fargo agent in Culver City and have him ship my trunk to me."

Alice frowned. "That could be risky if Trent is still looking for us. But I suppose you'll do it anyhow. It might not be safe for you to go alone though. I'll ask Mark to walk in with you."

Mark agreed to escort Eleonore into town and a few moments later walked down the main stairs to the hall with the girl at his side. Eleonore seemed determined to keep up her part as the French maid and carried on a chattering conversation in the same atrocious accent. She had cleared all traces of make-up from her face, except just enough to hide the traces of her black eye and, with her hair tucked up under the maid's cap would have been all but unrecognizable as the famous Madam Moustache.

Just as they reached the bottom of the stairs, the sturdy door opened and Humboldt stepped out. He beamed at Mark, the kind of look he reserved for important and influential people.

"Mark!" he boomed. "Come on in and meet my future son-in-law."

"Sure," Mark replied. "Wait here, Fifi." At the door he jerked his head towards the girl. "Lady Alice asked me to take her maid into town to do some shopping. So I said I would."

"I'll arrange for the buggy to be brought around for you, if you wish."

"Thanks," Mark replied sincerely, for he was a cowhand and never walked if he could avoid doing so.

"Come in then," said Humboldt and beckoned to his footman to give the orders. "I trust Lady Alice is comfortable."

"Why sure. She'll likely be down soon."

In the study Mark met Iris Humboldt and her fiancé. The girl stood about as tall as Eleonore and had much the same build, although not the same beautiful features, or slimming down at the waist. She looked pleasant enough, not too bright, although well educated. This showed in the short conversation Mark had with her and Gavin Stout, her fiancé. Maybe she was not bright, but she must have had something, for Stout looked like a good catch. He stood six foot tall, with good shoulders and tapering to a slim waist. His head and eyebrows were blond, while his face looked to have been shaven only a few minutes before and sported neither moustache nor side whiskers although these were fashionable back east. His clothes fitted him well and followed the latest eastern trend. His hand, when Mark took it, felt soft as if it had never done any work.

"Pleased to meet you, Mark," he said, giving the big Texan a searching glance.

"Have you been out west for long?" Mark asked, making conversation.

"This's my first trip," Stout replied, slipping an arm around Iris and squeezing her gently. "But we aim to make our home out here, don't we, darling?"

They talked on for a few moments. Stout had a ringing voice with a strong upper-class eastern accent and he seemed friendly enough. He started to tell Mark about the honeymoon trip they planned after the wedding, but the destination of which they meant to keep a secret.

"No sense in having everybody know where to find us, is there?" he chuckled.

At that moment he glanced through the door and saw Eleonore standing in the hall. Filled with female curiosity she had stepped into view to see what kind of a man met with Mrs. Humboldt's approval enough to be allowed to marry her daughter. She stood for a moment, looking hard at Stout.

A frown creased Stout's brow and an expression of fear almost flickered on his handsome face for a moment.

"I didn't know you had a new maid, darling," he said to Iris.

"We don't?"

"Then who—?"

"That's Lady Alice's maid," Mark put in.

He did not fail to notice the expression of relief flicker across the man's face, any more than he failed to see the fear which showed for a brief instant when Stout first saw Eleonore.

Before any more could be said, Humboldt returned with news that the buggy waited outside. Mark nodded to Stout and the girl, then left the room. Stout watched Eleonore pass out of sight, then turned back to talk with his fiancé once more.

Neither Mark nor Eleonore spoke as they left the grounds of Humboldt's residence. The two hard-cases were not in sight and nothing out of the way happened as they drove along the rutted road making for the main business area of the town, towards the Wells Fargo office and the jail.

"Who was the handsome man you talked with?" she asked.

"Me," Mark modestly replied.

"I meant the other one."

"That's the bridegroom-to-be," grinned Mark. "You handed him a shock coming out like that."

"His voice gave me one. I thought I should know it. In fact I'm sure I ought to know that man, but I can't place him."

Mark thought of that. He did not know why Stout should looked surprised, almost scared at seeing Eleonore. His thoughts on the subject were broken by Eleonore's hide searing comments on a friend who used trickery to make her sleep on the floor while the friend had a large and comfortable bed. The tirade lasted until they passed the Long Glass saloon.

"Say," Mark drawled. "You sure make a real fetching maid, though."

"Alice thinks so. With her 'fetch me this' and 'fetch me that'," groaned Eleonore. "Oooh! Why didn't you say I was an eccentric lady who liked to have her maid dressed up. Then I would have shown Alice a few things."

They were approaching the Wells Fargo office and Mark remembered something. "Say, if you need any money I can manage a stake until things go better for you."

"I have enough for my needs, thank you, *mon ami*," she replied. "I didn't lose everything at Culver Creek."

"But how did you carry it?" Mark asked, thinking back to the first night out of Culver Creek, when she came to tell him her life story.

"Zat is my beesiness, *m'sieur*," Eleonore answered with a saucy grin and a wink, reverting to her assumed French accent for the benefit of the loafers who stood before the office.

"And real nice business, too," Mark replied, jumping from his seat to help her down. "I'll collect you after I've seen the town marshal – Fifi."

She smiled curtsied and entered the office. Mark climbed back into the buggy and drove along the street to halt before the marshal's office. He left his buggy at the hitching rack and walked into the office. One look at the man behind the desk told Mark which of his stories he could tell. The man wore a town suit, just good enough in quality for him to be honest and even if Mark had not recognized him, he would have told the truth of the happenings in Culver Creek. He knew George Abbot well enough to expect a fair hearing and understanding of why he brought the two girls out of Trent's reach.

"Howdy, George," Mark said.

The old-timer's leathery face creased in a broad grin. "Howdy, Mark."

"Never thought to see you in a town like this."

In the old days George Abbott ran the law in bad, wide open towns. Before the war and for a couple of years after it, his name went out far as a straight and brave lawman. However, his age began to tell and he gave up handling the wild ones to look for safer employment. He drifted to Holbrock and took on the badge, finding a growing town which but rarely saw the wild horse-play of cowhands.

"Shucks, it's a living," George went on after explaining his reasons for ending in Holbrock. "Better'n getting shot down by a wild bunch of wild yahoos on a spree. What brings you here, you ain't just come along to see poor famous old George Abbott, now have you?"

Before Mark could reply the office door burst open and the two hard-cases came to a halt, the one with the deputy's badge pointing to Mark.

"That's him!" he yelled.

"Who, Brown?" asked Abbott calmly, though his eyes took on a frosty glint at the intrusion.

"The big jasper who come in with those two gals."

Mark swung to face the two men, not liking the look of either. He heard the marshal's chair scrape back and guessed Abbott had stood up ready to take cards. The marshal came around the side of his desk and halted by Mark.

"Where'd you come from, Mark?" he asked.

"The OD Connected," replied Mark, which was true - as far as it went.

"That'd mean you was a hell of a way off your line, happen you went to Culver Creek."

"I tell you he was with two women!" Brown, the deputy snapped.

"Knowing Mark here, that don't surprise me," drawled Abbott. "Who are they, boy?"

"Guests up at Humboldt's place. An English lady and her maid," Mark replied, which again, as far as it went, was the truth.

From the suspicious gleam in Brown's eyes he did not entirely believe Mark's story. He threw a glance at Abbott and waited for the marshal to make some reply to the big Texan's words.

"Look," Brown finally growled, when Abbott made no comment. "A big cowhand, fitting this jasper's description, and those two gals bust up the boss -

Trent's place in Culver Creek and I—"

"Thought in the fust place you said the gals took to fighting over who was to boss the big table," Abbott interrupted. "Don't sound likely that they'd be riding into town all friendly and sat on a wagon together, or however they come in."

Brown scowled. "Yeah, well the boss wants them gals finding and send—"

"Your boss don't run this town, office, or me!" Abbott barked.

"I'll soon get the truth out of him!" Brown snarled.

He took a step towards Mark, coming in his most threatening manner and dropping his hand towards his hip. Mark did not bother to clench his fist. He swung his right hand around in a flat-palm slap which caught Brown across the cheek and sprawled him clear across the office. Brown's pard gave an angry grunt and dropped his hand, then froze, for Mark's left hand dipped even as he slapped the deputy down. The long barrelled Army Colt came clear of leather and lined on the man, ending any moves he might be planning.

"All right," Mark said quietly, yet in a voice the other man would never forget. "I'm saying this just once, so both of you listen good to me. I came up here from the OD Connected and I didn't start any saloon brawl. If I see either of you in town comes nightfall I'll spit in your faces. You hear me?"

"I hear you," replied the second man, for Brown lay on the floor wondering what hit him.

"Then get your pard on his feet and out of here," Mark ordered.

The man helped Brown to his feet and steered him from the door. Abbott followed them out on to the sidewalk and spoke words of wisdom.

"You saddle up and ride. I'm not having you getting killed in my town and that would sure happen should you go up against Mark Counter in a fair fight. And, just happen you're fool enough to reckon on taking him any other way, me and his pappy were old pards, so I'll be standing 'side of him. And even if I weren't I sure wouldn't want to be the man who bushwhacked Mark Counter when Dusty Fog and the Ysabel Kid caught up with them. You go tell your boss there's no sign of the folks he wants here.''

He stood and watched the men. In his time as a lawman Abbott learned much about handling hardcases. He knew how they looked when they aimed to yell "calf-rope" before a better man. Brown and the other would not be staying on to trouble Mark, or Abbott would be surprised. He watched them slouch away and knew they would be out of Holbrock long before nightfall.

"Who are those pair at Humboldt's?" Abbott asked, when he returned to his office.

"Poker Alice and Madam Moustache."

''And Humboldt took them in?''

"He reckons they're Lady Alice Hatton-Green and her maid. Tell you one thing though, I called in at Culver Creek. That's where I met them.''

"Did, huh?"

"Sure. I'll tell you how it all happened.''

At the end of Mark's story, Abbott gave a low grunt. His expressed views on Trent as man and saloonkeeper came pungent and obscene. Nor did he for a minute doubt but that Mark told the full truth of what happened. He agreed that the two women were in no way to blame for what happened. Trent brought them together for the resulting fight and should have no cause to complain. Abbott chuckled immoderately as he heard how come the girls were now house guests at the Humboldt place.

"If he knew he'd throw a whingding," the marshal stated. "I'm looking forward to meeting Poker Alice at that fancy dinner tonight. Sure, I'm invited." He paused, studying Mark. "You seen the future son-in-law yet?"

"Why sure."

"What do you reckon to him?"

"I only saw him for a few minutes," Mark answered in a non-committal tone.

"Know what you mean. Why'd a handsome cuss like him, with money of his own, way he flashes it about, take a plain gal like young Iris?"

"They allow beauty's only skin deep," grinned Mark.

"Sure, especially when it's got a ten thousand dollar dowry skin and maybe another ten thousand in jewelry to go along."

Mark let out a whistle of surprise. "As much as that?"

"Yep. Give old Brenton credit, he sure dotes on that gal of his'n. She gets it all to make a start with. Taking most of it along with 'em on their honeymoon."

"You got a suspicious mind," grinned Mark.

"That's what keeps me alive," Abbott replied. "Whyn't you take a walk. I've got some important work to do."

"Sure, I'll pick Lady Alice's maid up from the Wells Fargo office. See you tonight – and don't snore too loud, the tax payers might hear you."

Leaving Abbott spluttering and trying to make an adequate reply, Mark stepped from the office and decided to walk along to the front of the Wells Fargo building as the local stage had just come into sight and the usual sort of crowd gathered to see it arrive. He could see no sign of Eleonore and this surprised him, for he expected her to be waiting for him.

The coach came to a rocking halt before the stage office and Mark strolled down the sidewalk towards the rear of the crowd. He saw a drummer leap down and hold open the door in a manner which showed, by his gallantry, that ladies of some kind must be aboard. He offered his hand to assist a flashily dressed blonde woman from the coach and an equally flashily dressed young redhead came to the open door standing waiting to be helped down. Her eyes went around the crowd with some interest, starting on the side away from where Mark stood.

A man turned hurriedly at the rear of the crowd and bumped full into Mark as he started to walk away. With a muttered apology the man stepped around Mark and strode off along the street at a good speed. Mark turned to watch him go, for as they came together he had felt the hard shape of a short-barrelled revolver under his coat.

Normally a man *not* carrying a gun would be an object of interest in Texas. For a man to carry one, even concealed under his coat, was completely ordinary – except that the man who bumped into Mark wore a black suit, round topped black hat, a black stock and white reversed collar. In fact the man who bumped into Mark wore the street clothes of a preacher belonging to a certain religious sect and Mark had never seen one who went armed about his work.

After watching the remarkable sight of a armed preacher swing away out of sight between two buildings, Mark turned once more to try and see Eleonore. He saw nothing of her, only the two new arrivals, clearly saloongirls in town to start working, headed along the sidewalk away from him. With the departure of the girls, the crowd broke up and went about their business, but still with no sign of Eleonore. Mark headed for the office, meaning to ask if the girl had left for he thought Brown and his pard might have seen her and taken a chance to grab her for return to Culver Creek.

Just as he reached the door of the office, Mark saw Eleonore come around the corner in a furtive manner, peering towards him first, then back to the chattering, laughing saloongirls, and their escort who passed along behind her.

"Whew!" gasped Eleonore, coming to Mark. "That was a close one."

"How do you mean?"

"First I come out of the office and almost walk into the Parson, I turn, take cover until I think he has gone away. Then come out and almost run into Ginger Lil. So I have to get back out of sight again quickly."

"They know you, huh?"

"Sure they know me. I caught the Parson trying to doctor a deck in a poker game and he was bounced around a little by the house muscle. So he sent his girl friend, Ginger Lil, after me and we tangled. My Mark, I don't think she has forgotten Madam Moustache yet, although her injuries have healed."

"Say, that Parson *hombre* wouldn't stand about five foot nine, have a thin, sharp face that looks like he's been drinking alkaline water for the first time?" asked Mark.

"He does."

"And he's real friendly with the red headed gal?"

"I did hear they quarrelled and split up," Eleonore answered. "He left her behind while she was recovering from the fight I had with her."

"That figgers. He took off like the devil after a yearling when he saw her come off the stage. You'd best tell me some about the Parson."

"I don't know too much. He travels the circuit working various confidence tricks, posing as a parson most of the time. I don't know why he is here."

Apart from deciding to warn Abbott of the man's presence in town Mark did nothing about the Parson. He took Eleonore back to the Humboldt house and left her while he went to make his preparations for the evening dinner and social gathering.

Later that evening the town and county's most influential people gathered at Humboldt's to be introduced to the guests of honor, Mark Counter and Lady Alice. It gave Mark much innocent amusement to watch the way Alice carried herself amongst the guests and he knew none of them doubted her or imagined her to be other than Lady Alice Hatton-Green. Much to Mark's surprise, Eleonore made her appearance clad in the best maid's dress, with a neat starched white hat and apron, tripping around the room, helping out Humboldt's over-worked staff and never putting a foot wrong, although her French-English accent did sound just a little too broad.

Mark saw that Gavin Stout paid a lot of attention to the girl when she made her first appearance, then seemed to decide she was harmless and joined the group of men who surrounded Lady Alice.

"Would you care for ze ponch, m'sieur?" asked Eleonore, carrying a small tray to where Mark stood by the door. She dropped her voice and a merry twinkle came to her eyes. "Old Ma Humboldt doesn't cotton to her future son-in-law getting friendly with Alice."

Mark glanced across the room to where Mrs. Humboldt entertained some of her friends. The woman kept throwing looks to where Alice held court and her fan flicked in angry jerks as she watched Stout laughing at something Alice said. To one side of the room Iris also stood watching, pouting a little as she saw her fiancé behaving in a manner he never used when in her presence.

Taking a glass of punch from Eleonore's tray, Mark strolled across the room to where he saw Abbott entering the room. He meant to warn the marshal about the mysterious gentleman known as the Parson. Before he reached Abbott, Mark caught a snatch of conversation between Humboldt and the local preacher as they sat at the edge of the room.

"He's a splendid fellow," the preacher remarked, carrying on with something started before Mark came within hearing distance. "Staying with us. We couldn't allow a brother of the cloth to put up at the hotel."

"You should have brought him along with you," Humboldt replied.

"I thought of it. But he came from taking a stroll just before we came here and said he had a headache. He retired to his room to rest."

"You could go around later and see if he feels up to making an appearance. Ah, Mark – you haven't met the Reverend Pooley yet, have you?"

So, what with being introduced to Pooley, then various other people, Mark did not get a chance to speak with the marshal. They were headed towards him when the butler came to Abbott's side, whispered in his ear and nodded to the door. Finishing his glass of punch, Abbott turned and left the room and the butler came to Humboldt.

"Mr. Abbott sends his apologies, sir," he said. "He has been called away to investigate a murder."

"M—murder?" Humboldt gulped. "Who was killed?"

"I couldn't say, sir," answered the butler and faded away.

Before Humboldt could say any more on the subject, he found the local preacher at his side and pointing to the door. Mark glanced in the direction of the door and saw the man Eleonore called the Parson walking towards Humboldt.

"Oh, oh!" said a voice at his elbow and he turned to find Eleonore at his side, holding a tray of drinks and looking towards the Parson. "If he recognizes me, he—"

"He can't expose you without giving himself away," Mark replied calmly. "But he'd best not see you. Go tell Alice you feel sick and want to get some air. I reckon she'll know."

Curtsying as if she had been offering Mark a drink, Eleonore turned and went to where Alice sat amongst a gathering of men. It took Alice one quick glance to know something was wrong and she came forward, passing through the men as if they did not exist.

"What is it, Fifi?" she asked.

To give her credit, Eleonore presented a masterly display of a woman about to be overcome by what polite folks termed the vapors. Instantly Alice expressed her concern, took the girl's tray and placed it on a small table, then escorted Eleonore from the room. Mrs. Humboldt saw this and followed, to come back and explain to the others how Lady Alice's maid had taken ill and the lady insisted on seeing her safely to her room. The incident did a lot of good for Alice's prestige and, on seeing this, Mrs. Humboldt's suspicions dulled, even though her future son-in-law appeared to be showing a great deal of interest in the beautiful English woman.

The gathering broke up fairly early, for the wedding would be held at eleven o'clock the following morning and Mrs. Humboldt wished to have her guests arrive on time, not to roll up at all hours, bleary eyed from a night's revelry.

Mark sat on his bed, removing his town shoes and wondering why men wore such things by choice. He heard the knock on his door and wondered who might be coming to see him, for he had been one of the last to retire, having been talking with Humboldt and a couple of local ranchers until the rest of the guests departed.

He rose, crossed the room and opened the door. Alice and Eleonore, both wearing their housecoats, entered quickly. He closed the door behind them and looked each girl up and down for a moment.

"No life stories tonight, gals," he grinned.

"This's more serious than that," Alice replied.

"Alice's right," agreed Eleonore. "Mark, Ginger Lil has been killed."

"Where?" Mark asked.

"It was she they fetched the marshal to see," Alice replied. "They found her in a livery barn, a knife in her back."

None of them spoke for a time, all busy with their own thoughts. Then Eleonore snapped her fingers.

"I have it. I remember where I saw Gavin Stout before!"

"Where?" Alice asked.

"In Newton. He married a rich storekeeper's daughter. They went on their honeymoon and he left her in Kansas City, but he did not leave the dowry, nor the jewelry she brought on her honeymoon. I remember just now. I also remember, he had dark hair and a moustache then. Of course, I look different also, so he does not remember me."

"Are you sure of this?" Mark asked.

"Very sure," replied Eleonore. "All the time since I first saw him I have been thinking, where did I last see this man, I studied him as I take the drink tray and at last I remember."

"If you're right—" began Mark.

"I am."

"That means the dear little Iris will have a rather short married life," Alice put in. "I wouldn't wish that even on her."

"There's one thing I don't get though," drawled Mark. "Why didn't the law get after him?"

"I don't know," Eleonore replied. "The storekeeper sold up in Newton and left soon after. What can we do, Mark?"

"Could try telling the Humboldts."

"And have Mrs. Humboldt suspect a trick to grab Gavin from her darling child," Alice put in. "She has been watching me most suspiciously all night. I thought he did it a bit brown myself, the way he hung around. Possibly he is thinking that Lady Alice Hatton-Green might be a better catch than little Miss Humboldt."

"Or his next catch after he gets rid of little Iris," Eleonore suggested. "We must do something, though. Do you think the Parson is connected with Stout?"

"Maybe, maybe not," Mark answered. "I'll drop a word in George Abbott's lil ear comes morning. I reckon the Parson might know something about that gal though. There's nothing we can do, except sleep on it."

Eleonore rose from where she had been sitting in a comfortable chair. "I can take a hint," she said. "Coming, Lady Alice?"

"Er, in a few minutes," Alice replied. "I've a few theories I want to discuss with Mark. No, you needn't stay, I can manage."

On entering their room, Eleonore laughed, removed the housecoat, put out the light and climbed into the comfortable bed, ignoring the mattress on the floor. Knowing what deep thinkers Mark and Alice were, she doubted if she would be disturbed until early morning.

"I trust you slept well, Lady Alice," said Mrs. Humboldt as she entered the dining-room and found Alice and Mark just finishing their breakfasts.

"Very well, thank you," Alice replied, neither blushing nor even glancing at Mark, for she knew the woman meant nothing more than polite conversation.

Before any more could be said, the butler entered and came straight to Mrs. Humboldt, followed by the Parson, whose face bore a look of sorrow.

"I'm afraid I have bad news for you, my dear Mrs. Humboldt," he said. "The Reverend Pooley has taken ill during the night. Nothing serious, but sufficient to keep him in bed all day. I thought I should bring you word of it so as to give you time to make other arrangements."

Mrs. Humboldt's face showed horror. "But – but, he can't be ill. The wedding is this morning and there isn't another preacher within – but you are a man of the church. Would you take the wedding ceremony?"

She turned her eyes to the Parson, who appeared to have been on the verge of leaving. He halted and faced her once more and held out a hand.

"If you wish, dear lady. I will attempt in my humble way to fill the Reverend Pooley's shoes."

Even as she opened her mouth to speak, Alice felt

Mark's foot come down on her toe. She closed her mouth quickly, with a barely concealed wince, watching his face and seeing the almost imperceptible shake of his head. She did not know what to make of this development and aimed to learn about it quickly.

"Excuse me, please," she said. "Are you coming, Mark?"

Her tone meant, "Either come and explain or I spill all I know and chance the consequences."

Mark rose, nodded to the Parson and followed Alice from the dining-room and up to enter her room. Eleonore still lay in the bed and she grinned, then lost her grin and sat up.

"What is it?" she asked.

After Mark told her of the latest development Eleonore snapped, "Why didn't you speak?"

"Because it's your word against his," Mark replied. "And happen he spooks and runs from here he's left free to pull the same game in some other place. Even if Stout gets lost in the deal he can easy find another good looking feller to take on. Then some more innocent gals'll suffer."

"But he killed Ginger Lil!"

Mark studied the dark-haired girl for a moment. "You see him do it?"

"Of course I didn't."

"Then you can't prove that either. Sure it looks likely he did. He knew her and happen she recognized him she might want paying too much to keep her mouth shut. Or she might be after his scalp for running out on her and wouldn't take pay. So he quietened her. But we can't prove it."

All this time Alice had been pacing up and down the room. She came to a halt and faced the other two.

"I've an idea that might work."

She told her idea and the other two exchanged glances. It looked like a real risky game, but happen it worked would save Iris from a terrible mistake. Mark gave his approval of it and Eleonore shrugged, then agreed to take her part.

"Get to it, gals," Mark drawled. "I've just time to see George Abbott before the marrying starts."

Mark learned little from Abbott. The old marshal knew his business, but admitted frankly to being puzzled. From Ginger Lil's blonde friend he learned that the girl came to Holbrock looking for work and the blonde travelled along, being tired of her last place. Lil never mentioned knowing anybody in Holbrock and the girl could think of nobody in their last town who might have hated Lil enough to kill her. They left their rooming house to walk to the saloon just as it grew dark but halfway to the Long Glass Lil said she had forgotten her bag and would go to collect it. The blonde went on to start work and had been in the Long Glass in full view of the customers all night, also a couple of loafers had seen the girls part, so Lil had been alive when the blonde last saw her, which let the blonde out as a suspect.

"Why all the interest, Mark?" asked Abbott.

"Let's just say I'm curious."

"Yeah? Waal, was you a mite smaller I'd say let's just say you're lying."

"All right then. Set fast and listen," drawled Mark.

On hearing Mark's story Abbott's first inclination was to rush out and arrest both Stout and the Parson. However, it took him a bare ten seconds to see how little chance he would having of making any charge stick, so he settled down to hear the plan Mark, Alice and Eleonore formed. At the end he gave a low grunt which might have meant anything and agreed to let Mark play the game his way.

Mrs. Humboldt had worries. Never a good organizer, she managed to get herself in quite a state before the ceremony. She wanted to see to the seating of the guests and also wished to help her daughter dress. So she felt relieved when Alice came with the offer of helping Iris to get ready, allowing Mrs. Humboldt freedom to attend to her other affairs.

After Mrs. Humboldt left the room Eleonore closed and locked the door, an action which went unnoticed by Iris who had worked herself into a state of near panic waiting for someone to help her dress. Alice eased the girl into a chair and looked down at her.

"We want to tell you something first," she said.

Quietly and without showing any emotion, Alice told of Gavin Stout's previous marriage, of the fake preacher who would officiate at this wedding. When she finished she saw at a glance that she could have saved her time and put the other idea into practice, for Iris made the reply she expected.

"I don't believe a word of it. I saw you making up to Gavin last night. You want him for yourself."

"My dear girl," Alice replied. "I assure you I've no interest in Gavin Stout other than preventing him from hurting you."

"It's a lie!" Iris gasped. "It's all lies. Papa got in touch with Gavin's bankers in Hartford and they told us about him."

"And who told you how to find Gavin's bankers?" Eleonore asked.

"Gavin did. He had nothing to hide," answered the girl, her voice rising higher. "Now get out of my house. I'll tell—"

She thrust herself to her feet, shoving between the two women. Eleonore gave a shrug, caught her by the arm and turned her.

"Doesn't she look beautiful?" sniffed Mrs. Humboldt, watching the white clad shape come along the aisle on her husband's arm.

The guests all looked. Mark Counter, on the front row, watched everything and wondered which of their plans had been put in operation. He studied the veiled face for a moment, but could see nothing of the features below that which might help him know. Alice had appeared shortly before the notes of the Wedding March rose from the harmonium at the side of the room. She nodded to Mark as she took her seat, but could say nothing.

Looking severe and very holy, the Parson conducted the ceremony. He must have learned his subject well, for he made no mistakes through the entire business of marrying Gavin Stout to the veiled girl. At last the ring slipped on to a plump finger and the Parson said:

"You may now kiss the bride."

With a well simulated self-conscious smile Stout lifted the veil as the girl turned towards him. He gave a sudden horrified gasp and staggered back, his face suddenly ashy and ugly. The watching guests let out a cross between a gasp, cry and moan. Mrs. Humboldt screeched, half rose from her chair and then collapsed in a faint.

"Hello, Parson," said the bridal-clad Eleonore calmly. "Remember me?"

With a snarled out curse the Parson took a hurried pace back, staring at the white clad figure before him. Then his hand shot under his coat towards the butt of the five shot Colt House Pistol hidden beneath it.

"Hold it!"

Mark Counter had come to his feet as the veil raised, guessing what must be happening, that Eleonore, not Iris, stood before the Parson. His well tailored cutaway jacket would have shown a bulge if he tried to carry one or both of his big Army Colts, but a Remington Double Derringer took up little room and could easily lie concealed without attracting attention.

Whirling around, the Parson saw his danger. He tried to swing the Colt towards Mark but the big Texan reacted with the speed his name might have become famous for had he not lived under the shadow of the Rio Hondo gun wizard Dusty Fog. Twice the Remington belched flame and cracked out before the Parson's gun came full around. Mark shot in the manner of a trained lawman, shot the only way he dare under the circumstances, for an instant kill. He threw two bullets into the Parson, secure in the knowledge that the light charge and small barrels of the Double Derringer did not raise sufficient power to send the bullets clean through his man. Twice the Parson rocked as lead hit him. His gun fell from his fingers and he went down in a limp pile on the floor.

Even before the Parson made his desperate play, while the other man's gun came clear, Stout turned and dashed down the aisle. Most of the watching crowd were still too stunned to think clearly but George Abbott sprang forward. He did not wear a gun, but leapt at Stout and was knocked aside. A moment later Stout felled the amazed butler, having heard shots and guessing his partner would not be following. He raced to the front doors, through them, turning to grab the key, saw Mark Counter coming after him and closed, then locked the doors on the outside. That would slow down the pursuit for a few moments and a buggy with a fast horse stood waiting in case a hurried departure became necessary. Without a thought for his partner, not caring whether the Parson lived or died, Stout leapt into the buggy and untangled the reins, then reached for the whip.

After shooting the Parson, Mark dropped his empty weapon and raced down the aisle in pursuit of Stout. Luckily for them none of the guests got in the way, for Mark intended to get the man. Men shouted, women screamed, Abbott cursed and tried to untangle himself but Mark ignored any of it. He saw the departure and heard the click of the lock. Mark did not even slacken his pace or break his stride. At the last moment he ducked one shoulder and hurled himself with all his strength into the stout doors, bursting them open as if they had been made of matchwood. He saw the buggy, saw Stout in it and lunged forward.

The whip in Stout's hands lashed out at Mark, only once, for Mark reached the buggy, his hands clamped on the spokes of the wheel and with a tremendous surging heave he threw it over on to its side. Stout howled as he shot out and lit down on the ground.

He came up fast but Mark was on him before he could even think of defence or flight. In his time Stout had been in more than one rough-house brawl and thought he knew how to defend himself. He stood no chance at all against a cold, grim, angry Mark filled with a decent man's hate of all Stout stood for. With all his anger Mark lost none of his skill and Stout suffered the more because of it. Iron hard fists, powered by giant muscles, ripped into Stout's face and body. He felt his nose crushed and spread over his face, his level white teeth break and his body take smashing blows. Then he went down and all became black and still.

"You got a real mean streak in you, boy," Abbott remarked, coming from the door of the house. "Happen you hadn't stopped in ten – fifteen minutes I reckoned on stopping you. He'll never look pretty again, that's for sure."

"Take him to jail, George," Mark replied. "I'd best go inside again."

In the big room the wedding guests stood chattering, pointing and talking. Mark entered and the talk died down, the guests waited to hear an explanation of what they had seen.

"It worked, Mr. Humboldt," Alice said suddenly, in a loud and carrying voice even before Mark could speak. "Thanks to you we caught him."

She had watched Humboldt ever since Eleonore revealed herself. The man's face showed sickness and hurt as he guessed what must be happening. Alice guessed at the feelings of the pompous man who prided himself on his judgment of character, who had his friends believing in his omnipotence and found himself shown as a fool who allowed a confidence trickster to fool him. He could hardly stand the humiliation, the expectancy of jeers to come. Alice took pity on him, she thought fast, came up with a possible way out, used it and hoped Mark and Eleonore would go along with her in its use.

"My fellow operative and I," she said, indicating Eleonore who had removed the bridal veil and was helping revive Mrs. Humboldt, "have been after the Parson and Stout for some time. We trailed them here and told Mr. Humboldt of their activities, hoping he would stop the wedding. With a courage I can only describe as magnificent, Mr. Humboldt insisted we let the marriage carry on so as to trap them both red-handed and prevent some other girl being victimized by them. We all apologize for bringing you here, but you will all understand that it was necessary and I'm sure none of you can object to helping remove a couple of dangerous and heartless men, probably saving heartache and distress to other young, innocent girls."

Alice hit at the crowd in a manner they could not pass over. They might not like the idea of being tricked, but who would dare to say so in public when word of the reason for their being invited came out. Alice knew human nature, knew the kind of people who might object would also be the kind to see how their social standing would be enhanced by having it known that they helped trap two men who preyed on innocent girls.

Looking across the room Alice met Humboldt's eyes and she would never forget the look of gratitude in them. At the same moment she remembered Iris still remained upstairs, bound with her own stockings and gagged.

"Who are you?" asked one of the guests.

"We operatives aren't allowed to disclose our true identity."

"Pinkertons!" whispered a man, reaching the conclusion Alice hoped he would.

That evening a small group gathered in Humboldt's

study. Mark, Humboldt, the two lady gamblers and Abbott sat around discussing the happenings of the day. In more ways than one Humboldt had cause to be grateful for the arrival of Poker Alice and Madam Moustache. Not the least reason was the way Alice talked with his daughter and finally persuaded Iris everything happened for the best. The girl would be sent east to forget and time would heal the ache she felt.

"Stout talked plenty, when he come around," Abbott remarked. "Seem like him and the Parson run this game five times already. Always use the same address in Hartford, there's a feller at it answers the letters for them, when the father wrote to check on Stout. The Parson slipped something in Pooley's coffee last night, nothing serious, just enough to keep him off his feet until after the ceremony."

"But why did they do that?" Humboldt asked.

"Look at it this way. Your gal gets married by a real preacher, that's legal and only a divorce in the courts can bust it. Which attracts attention to what's happened, might bring the law in. So they figure that after Stout dumps the gal they let her father know the wedding was a fake. So he now has an unmarried daughter and most likely'll let it go rather than admit that he's been made a fool of. In time, when it's all blown over, or maybe because he's moved to another place where he's not known, he can get the gal married again and not risk divorce, or bigamy. It's happened each time they played it."

"Who killed Ginger Lil?" Eleonore asked.

"Stout lays it on the Parson and I believe him," Abbott replied. "She'd traced the Parson here and wanted half of the take. Stout reckons the Parson got him to one side last night and told him that he'd closed Lil's mouth for good."

Soon after the meeting broke up, with Humbolt showering his thanks on all concerned for their help. In a few weeks' time he would most likely have forgotten that they helped and be sure that his own astute nature brought about the successful conclusion of the affair.

Mark walked with Alice and Eleonore in the garden shortly after dark. He slipped an arm around each girl's waist and they stood by the gate looking towards the lights of the town.

"You did the right thing, Alice," he said. "Telling the story the way you did, clearing Humboldt."

· "They could call you 'Lady' Alice all the time," Eleonore agreed. "I am proud to know you, Alice."

"And I'm proud to know you, Eleonore," Alice smiled. "But don't you ever try to take my table from me again."

"Your table!" Eleonore squealed. "Why you—"

Holding them apart Mark laughed, then they laughed. He leaned forward and brought their heads together, whispering something in their ears. Two startled faces looked at him.

"Both of us?" Alice gasped.

"What a man!" sighed Eleonore.

All in all Mark was not sorry to ride back towards the OD Connected at dawn. He left Alice and Eleonore preparing to travel from Holbrock and hoped he might run across one or both again in the future. Right now he was headed home and did not care – it sure took it out of a man to tell his life story to two gals, especially two gals like Poker Alice and Madam Moustache, in one night.